INSIDE OUTSIDERS

Eileen Wiard

INSIDE OUTSIDERS

Copyright © 2013 by Eileen Wiard. All rights reserved.

Published by Nighthawk Press.

Printed in the United States of America.

ISBN: 978-0615892863

Library of Congress Control Number: 2013951389

Cover photograph: Lenny Foster, Living Light Gallery, Taos, New Mexico (www.lennyfoster.com)

Cover design: Lesley Cox, FEEL Design Associates, Taos, New Mexico (www.feeldesignassociates.com)

Author photograph: Stephen Wiard

Interior design: Barbara Scott, Final Eyes, Taos, New Mexico (www.finaleyes.net)

Type is set in ITC Legacy.

Contact the author at insideoutsidersthebook@gmail.com.

NIGHTHAWK PRESS

TAOS, NEW MEXICO

www.nighthawkpress.com

Acknowledgments

I am indebted to Susan Eaton's research in *Boston's Other Busing Story,* the truth-telling of Richard Wright's *Black Boy,* Maya Angelou's *I Know Why the Caged Bird Sings,* Alice Walker's *The Color Purple,* Toni Morrison's *The Bluest Eye;* to PFLAG in Taos; the F.I.R.S.T. grant funding a middle-school health project that introduced me to this age group and their concerns; and the Safe Schools Project at the Department of Education in Massachusetts, which prioritized lesbian, gay, bisexual and transgender students and helped teachers understand and protect them; to students and fellow teachers in schools too numerous to mention; to writing teachers Minrose Gwin, Summer Wood, Bonnie Lee Black, Gregory Martin, Robert Wilder, Sean Murphy and Dorothy Allison.

I thank the Helene Wurlitzer Foundation of Taos, New Mexico, which first recognized the writer in me, and Michael Knight, who let me stay there long enough to make Taos my home; the Society of the Muse of the Southwest (SOMOS), which nurtures the writing and reading community here; the Taos Summer Writers Conference, sponsored by the University of New Mexico; Bonnie Lee Black for her suggestions that have improved this story; Barbara Scott for her fastidious copy-editing and design work; Lesley Cox for her book-cover-design artistry; Lenny Foster for capturing Crystal's spirit in Malaika Yambire; Malaika for her willingness to share her beauty and her soul; and Rebecca Lenzini of Nighthawk Press, who gave my story a home.

On a personal note, I am grateful to my husband, Steve, who is my champion and the first gentle reader of this story; Jess Mullen, my daughter, life teacher and inspiration; to Mari Tara, Betsy Wall, Inky Hvistendahl, Merilee Trenholm, and Laura Lynch, who listen to me with compassion and insight; to Lori Howes, whose heart is forever entwined with mine; to Virginia Kovaleski and Sharon Kalinowski, my sisters, who have known me longer than anyone; and to all the people I've met at meetings in church basements, libraries and round rooms, who taught me that I didn't have to be an outsider all my life by welcoming me into their hearts and showing me a different path.

May we all find our way inside to the lives we are meant to live.

Eileen Wiard

INSIDE OUTSIDERS

Eileen Wiard

Chapter One

"Shut *up,* Tawana," Crystal said.

"I'm only sayin'," Tawana said.

"Well, stop sayin'. I don't wanna hear it, whatever you're sayin'. You don't know what you're talkin' about."

"I do so know what I'm sayin', girl."

"And don't call me 'girl.' I ain't your girl."

Crystal looked at Tawana who was starting to laugh, and she gave in to it. The two girls had known each other for over a year now, and some things were just not worth fighting over.

Crystal was like Tawana's opposite in so many ways. Crystal had thick, long braids and big brown eyes with golden glints. Her skin was toffee-colored because her mother's father was white. Tawana, on the other hand, was from the island of Jamaica, and her skin was dark and rich. Her accent wasn't as strong as her mother's, because she'd been living in America all her life, but when she smiled, the whites of her teeth were shiny and made her seem happier, somehow. Plus, the girl just couldn't stop giggling.

The first time they met, they didn't even like each other. But Crystal and Tawana rode in on the COMBOS bus together every morning from Dorchester, in the heart of Boston, an hour earlier than any of the white kids in this school. They did this for the privilege of getting a good education at Gilmore Middle School, one of the best public school systems in the Commonwealth of Massachusetts. Tawana could hear her mother's voice saying that to everyone they knew. In their middle school of eleven hundred students, only forty were black, like Crystal and Tawana. They almost *had* to be friends.

The two girls lived several streets apart, which was a lot in a city the size of Boston. You knew your neighborhood—the good parts, the not-so-good parts, and you might not see the other COMBOS kids except in school and on the bus. Crystal knew that Gilmore was a good zip code to go to school in. There were others, too, like Lexington, that tried to do something to counter the horrible mess that was Boston when schools were forced to integrate back in the seventies. Busing in the cities had meant shipping one bunch of poor kids, either white or black, into another neighborhood with the opposite color kids, to make things more equal. Unfortunately, even though the black neighborhoods always had worse schools, the white schools weren't really that much better. Riots erupted, and blood was shed. It was a bitter time.

So when the COMBOS program started, short for "Communities of Boston," it was trying to do something to help kids in those inner city neighborhoods have a fighting chance. Once a family of kids was accepted into the COMBOS program, parents had to be supportive, and if the kids did well, they could go all the way through twelve grades in the same system. The idea was, they'd make friends, get the same educational challenges and resources, and apply to similar colleges as the kids who lived in the wealthy suburbs around Boston.

Right at this moment, Crystal and Tawana were on the bus, heading to school in Gilmore about an hour away. They sat together every day on that bus, about halfway back, and were on the same "team" in the middle school. The school was divided into four teams, where the students would share a language arts teacher, a math teacher, a science teacher, and a social studies teacher. The rest of the time, they'd share from a pool of art, music, and computer technology teachers. It meant something to belong to a team. Mostly it made the school seem just a little bit smaller.

"Did you do your social studies homework?" Tawana asked.

"Yes. I always do my homework, and the answer is no, you can't have it."

"Crystal, why are you so mean?"

"I'm not mean. Why should I give you my work just 'cause you're too lazy to do your own?"

"I'm not lazy. I don't get it."

Crystal saw Tawana looking down at her shoes, a new pair she'd just gotten at Payless last weekend. They probably hurt her feet, but boy, did Crystal like those shoes!

"So ask the teacher, Dummy. That's what she's there for." Crystal's voice was a little softer now. This was a conversation they'd had many times.

"She hates me. You know she hates me. She'll just yell at me for not paying attention. She'll say,

'Tawana, if you were listening, you'd know how to do that.' I ain't gonna look stupid in front of everybody."

"Yeah, you do look bad when she catches you daydreaming."

"I can't help it. That class is so boring."

"Every class is boring to you. How are you ever gonna graduate from this school if you don't start tryin'?"

Tawana explained that she did try, but being out two days the week before had put her way behind. And now she was lost.

When Crystal suggested signing up for extra help, Tawana resisted that, too. There was only one late bus back to Boston for the COMBOS kids, and going for extra help meant missing the only after-school activity Tawana enjoyed — cheerleading.

"Well, that's what I would do," said Crystal.

"I guess that's why they make vanilla and chocolate, right?" said Tawana.

"You calling me vanilla just cause I do my homework?"

"Maybe on the inside. 'Cause on the inside, you're opposite me, Crystal. And there's no way this Jamaican is gonna ever pass for vanilla." They caught each other's eyes again and laughed louder than ever.

"You got that right," said Crystal, as she pulled out her copy of *To Kill a Mockingbird* and started reading where she'd left off. Next thing she knew, Tawana was turning around to the back of the bus, yelling at her friend Derek. Derek was a seventh grader on their team, too, and was pretty good looking, if Crystal cared about that sort of thing. She caught a glimpse of the trees turning from green to orange and red and yellow. She really liked this time of year.

Gilmore had its good points. Crystal never had to worry about getting knifed on the way to or from school, like kids in her neighborhood did. When she compared notes with her cousins, she was already reading books they were just being assigned, and they were in high school. Unless you were lucky enough to pass the exams for Boston Latin by the time you were in seventh grade, school in Boston was a big waste of time.

But Crystal paid a price. Her Dorchester friends made fun of the way she talked — "all white and uppity"— and said she dressed white just to fit in. Little did they know that the kids at Gilmore made fun of her, too. Her parents couldn't afford to buy clothes at Russell's in Gilmore Center, so they shopped at Russell's Basement, where Crystal's mom worked, and the Gilmore kids knew her outfits were last year's extras. Plus, the hours she spent on the bus made it nearly impossible to have friends to do things with at home in the neighborhood until summertime, and by then it was hard to catch up. A lot happens between September and June.

Crystal was the older of two daughters in her family, and everyone was counting on her to make something of herself. She liked to read, which was a good way to spend all that time riding back and forth on the bus. She did well in school, even though it didn't make her friendship with Tawana any easier. Crystal didn't understand why Tawana goofed off so much. School was easy. Why was Tawana being so stubborn?

All Crystal had to do was keep up with her homework, so she didn't know what it was like to have to try, the way Tawana used to try, and only get Cs for her effort. Crystal really believed that school was fair; that if you put in the effort, you would get good results.

In her mind, Tawana was just boy crazy. It's all she wanted to talk about — the cute boys at Gilmore, who was going out with whom, and who broke up this week. Dancing and now cheerleading were the only things Tawana wanted to do, the only things she was willing to work hard at.

Crystal didn't like the kids Tawana was hanging out with this year, many of them white. They had a bad attitude, talked back to teachers, did a little shoplifting; but compared with the trouble going on in her own neighborhood, Crystal could see Tawana still felt like a good kid. Maybe that's because she hardly ever got caught.

"Why don't you come with us today at lunch time?" Tawana asked her.

"What, sneaking around in Gilmore Center? That's just stupid, Tawana. You stick out like a sore thumb. You're gonna get caught, and then what?"

"Don't be such a scaredy-cat. I've never been caught once. Why should I now? Besides, it's fun. Danny will be there, and Suzanne, and Jamie..."

"No way I'm gonna do that. You go have fun with all those rich white kids."

"They're not rich, Crystal! They're okay, really. You could be friends with them, too, if you stopped being such a goody-goody."

"I'm not a goody-goody. I'm just not stupid."

"Suit yourself."

Crystal sighed, tired of trying. Why did she have to be the one to obey all the rules? Maybe Tawana would get in trouble, but so far, she'd been pretty lucky. Maybe her friend was right. Maybe Crystal shouldn't be missing out on all the fun.

Was it really better to be safe than sorry? Crystal was beginning to wonder. Still, she didn't like those kids. They were morons. She didn't trust them, but she missed having lunch with Tawana.

Soon enough, the yellow bus turned the corner onto the tree-lined street that meant they'd arrived. Everyone got off and climbed up the stairs to Gilmore Middle School for another day. Crystal was happy for the distraction of other students heading to their lockers. She and Tawana followed all the other kids heading to the seventh grade on the B Team wing of the school. Crystal loved to get rid of some of her belongings — the heavier math and science books — and hang up her sweat shirt on the hook in her locker. She'd decorated it with some pictures of her family and made room on the top for her favorite Beanie Baby, a gray elephant named Peanut.

Ms. Jones, the COMBOS advisor, walked by and gave her a big hello. "Crystal, are you ready? Today is barreling on in here, and I don't know what's on this train heading your way."

"Yes, Ms. Jones. I'm as ready as I'm ever gonna be."

"Good, and how about you, Tawana?"

"Me? I'm never ready, but I'm here," said Tawana.

Ms. Jones made her way down the hall, greeting every one of her COMBOS kids by name. She was an added benefit to the COMBOS program, a special advisor who was herself African American and lived in Roxbury, another inner-city section of Boston. She was the only black grown-up in the whole school. In fact, she was the only teacher of color. Ms. Jones' whole job was to take care of the COMBOS kids in the middle school. She would run interference for them if things got difficult, and she'd help them to get along in this school and take full advantage of their chance at a better education.

Her office was on the first floor of the building, right next to the main office, but she made herself visible whenever the students were milling around, before and after classes, during lunch, and especially at the beginning and ending of the day. If there was going to be trouble, that's usually when it happened.

Chapter Two

"Gomez is gonna catch you eating that banana, Tawana. Man, I could smell that thing as soon as you got on this bus." Crystal couldn't help laughing though.

"Well, I didn't have time to eat any breakfast, and I'm starving, and..."

Crystal couldn't hear what else her friend was trying to say because she had crammed half the banana into her mouth.

"No eating on the bus!" shouted Mrs. Gomez, the bus driver.

Crystal and Tawana burst out laughing, and bits of banana mush came shooting out of Tawana's mouth like an unchecked sneeze.

"That's it. I've had it with you kids. I'm writing you up for breaking the rules again, Tawana. Don't you know how lucky you are to be riding on this COMBOS bus, to be going to school in Gilmore? Well, you'll just have to find another way to get here next week."

"A whole week? You're going to punish me for a week for eating breakfast? That's not right," Tawana said. She was just getting started.

"Shut *up,* Tawana. You're just gonna make it worse," said Crystal, jabbing her friend in the side with her elbow.

"I don't care. I hate her. I hate Gilmore. That school's like a jail."

"Don't do it, I'm tellin' you, you better shut your mouth right now," said Crystal.

But Tawana was off. There was no stopping her once she got going. Mrs. Gomez ignored her and started writing notes in her daily log. The two friends rode the rest of the way in dread of what would happen next.

As soon as they got into the building, Crystal went along while Mrs. Gomez dragged Tawana to the COMBOS office to speak with Ms. Jones.

"Am I hearing this right, Tawana?" asked Ms. Jones.

"What's the point? You already heard her side of the story. Whatchou need mine for?"

"That attitude is not helping you, Tawana. Did you or did you not eat a banana on the bus this morning?"

"You know I did. I tried to eat it while I was waiting for the bus on the corner but it came too early, and I didn't have a chance to finish."

"So what are you supposed to do when that happens?" asked Ms. Jones.

"I know, I know, I'm supposed to wait till I get to school, then come here and eat breakfast in your office. But I was starving, Ms. Jones."

"Well, there's nothing I can do about that. We've got rules, and you broke one of them— again—and Mrs. Gomez says she won't even see your face on that bus till next week. Now I have to call your mother and tell her, and believe me, I'm not looking forward to that."

"I'll call her. I did it," said Tawana, sheepish now at the thought of her mother's reaction to having to drive her to school for a week.

"Couldn't you try to make it just a couple days, please Ms. Jones?" Tawana asked. "I won't do it again. I promise."

"I can't change her mind, but a sincere apology to Mrs. Gomez might work," Ms. Jones said.

Tawana sighed, rolled her eyes, and walked over to the bus driver, who was sitting in the main office. "Mrs. Gomez?"

"Yes, what do you want now?"

"I want to apologize. I know I shouldn't be eating on the bus; I was just really hungry and in a big hurry this morning. I'm sorry. You have every right to kick me off the bus for a week, but that doesn't really punish me. It punishes my mother. I'm gonna call her and all, but would you consider a shorter time than a week?"

"All I put up with from you kids, and there you sit, just laughing at me. You think this is easy, what I do every day?"

"No, Ma'am," said Tawana. "I wasn't laughing at you. Crystal just said something, and I was trying to answer her with a mouthful of banana, and she couldn't understand me. And then you said, 'No eating on the bus,' and I just couldn't control myself. I'm sorry. Really, we weren't laughing at you."

Mrs. Gomez narrowed her eyes and looked at Tawana with her head tilted just a little. "Well, your mother is a fine woman and a friend of mine. If you promise never to break the 'no eating' rule again, or any of the other ones, for that matter, I'll say just two days instead of five. But I'm warning you, Tawana..."

"I know Mrs. Gomez. Thank you, thank you so much."

Tawana left the office and walked down the hall. Crystal was waiting there for her by the lockers, and Tawana told her about how she got Mrs. Gomez to agree to two days instead of a whole week. Crystal said, "You're mom's gonna be sooo mad at you."

"I know." Tawana looked down guiltily. "Just last week, she was complaining about how she didn't get home from her job at Woolworth's till seven at night, and couldn't I help get out the clothes for my little brother, and how was she going to get everyone up and out of bed by five all by herself. I'm dead."

Unfortunately, that was not the last of it. Derek couldn't resist telling the entire homeroom what had happened on the bus, so all the kids knew that Tawana, who happened to be one of the darker-skinned COMBOS kids, was caught eating a banana.

When Derek told the story, he romped around the room like a monkey, his fingers scratching under his arms, jumping all over. That's what Tawana and Crystal walked into right before the morning announcements came over the public address system.

"Shut *up,* Derek," Tawana said. "If there's a stupid gorilla in this school, is sure isn't me."

"You won't see me eatin' no banana, I'll tell you that, Tawana Banana," he said, pronouncing her name to rhyme with the fruit.

Crystal could see her friend's eyes filling up, her throat swallowing hard, trying to keep her tears from spilling all over everything. She should not cry in front of this homeroom. Crystal knew it hurt Tawana all the worse because Derek was one of them, just another kid from Boston.

Crystal jumped in as soon as she could, but it was too late.

"Derek," she said, "You don't know what you're talking about. Look at yourself. I can't believe you."

Derek acted as if she wasn't even there. Finally, Ms. Lewis, their homeroom teacher, who had been out in the corridor talking to someone, came back into the room, putting an end to the painful moment. Derek stopped his antics abruptly and swaggered over to his desk, smiling broadly at his audience.

Crystal thought, why did he do that stupid stuff? Didn't Derek know how ridiculous it made not just Tawana look, but all of them, Derek included? Crystal hated that he ignored her. She hoped he'd heard her but figured he probably was too caught up in showing off to listen.

As much as Tawana deserved to be punished for eating on the bus, she did not deserve that betrayal by Derek. Crystal couldn't even look Tawana in the face. When something like that happened, it affected all of them. White people, they didn't care. Crystal didn't trust any of them, not even the Blaines, her host family since elementary school. They just didn't get it.

The bell finally rang, and Crystal drifted out into the hallway with everyone else. She had a heaviness that she carried with her, though. It started in her chest, right underneath her heart, and it stayed there all day.

* * *

When the bus dropped her off, Crystal felt tired, but her feet took her up the street and up the stairs as fast as they always did. She couldn't wait to plop herself down on the couch and put her feet up. What a day.

She shook her head, thinking about the morning's events, starting with the banana on the bus, and realized that she never really felt safe until she got home. As much as Gilmore Middle

School was her school, she felt like she didn't quite belong there.

She remembered the first time she met the Blaines, her host family, just as she was about to start third grade in Gilmore. Her parents brought her to Gilmore South Elementary School to participate in the open-house event. The idea was for each COMBOS student to pair up with a host family from Gilmore who had children the same age, so each COMBOS kid would know someone from Gilmore when they started in September.

There were snacks and a few circle games to learn names and have some fun together. This way, if something happened in school and COMBOS kids needed to go home, or to stay late, after the bus left, or in the case of any emergency, there'd be a Gilmore contact to act like another family to take care of things till the COMBOS kids' parents could pick them up.

Judy Blaine was in third grade, too. Especially that first year, Crystal thought it was neat to have a white friend at school. Judy was nice to her and invited her to play with her friends at recess. Mrs. Blaine was always inviting Crystal to come for dinner whenever she wanted to, but it wasn't really practical. She did go to Judy's birthday party in November that year, and in fourth grade, too.

But as she and Judy got older, their interests changed. Judy wanted to be a cheerleader. She took gymnastics. She thought Crystal's Beanie Babies were babyish. Crystal always had a book with her, and she started to say no when Judy invited her to play tag and other games with her friends. Crystal didn't like to sweat.

When Judy started talking about going on a diet to look better in her leotard, Crystal knew it was all over. Crystal had put on some weight, but her mom had explained that it was all about puberty, and how most girls put on a few pounds before their bodies started the bigger changes. Crystal wasn't about to stop eating chocolate-chip cookies just because of that.

But that was just one of the ways they were different. Judy never did invite Crystal to sit at her table in the cafeteria. And there was the time Crystal invited Judy to come to her birthday party in fourth grade. Judy's parents called to explain that no, it was too dangerous for them to drive in the dark in that neighborhood.

Her family lived in Dorchester, in a nice three-story house with a yard that even had a vegetable garden. Crystal's mom was really proud of their home, and Crystal felt safe there, surrounded by her family. Her grandmother lived on the first floor, her cousins with their new baby lived in the second-floor apartment, and Crystal's immediate family lived on the top floor. Each floor had a front and back porch. She liked the top floor best, because it got lots of sunlight, and the songbirds who made their nests in the trees in the backyard sang to Crystal every day, in the morning and at supper-time. She loved where she lived.

Why did white people think that all black peopled lived in a ghetto? Judy's parents didn't even know enough to be embarrassed at what they were saying, or to say the were sorry for insulting them that way. Crystal felt she would never understand white people. She wished her skin was so thick they couldn't hurt her feelings anymore.

Once, in fourth grade, when Crystal was playing at Judy's house after school, Judy's grandmother was watching them. When they complained about being bored, the older Mrs. Blaine turned the radio up, stopped at a hip-hop station and said, "Why don't you dance? I'll bet Crystal *loves* to dance, don't you Crystal?" She turned and smiled with a big silly grin at her granddaughter and Crystal.

Crystal hated hip-hop music. She liked the oldies, mostly. Her mother said it used to be called bubble-gum music in the seventies. Crystal hated to be lumped in with all the other black people, as if all people with brown and black skin had only one brain filled with the same thoughts; one pair of eyes with the same vision; one tongue with taste buds that liked all the same foods. How stupid to think that way.

Crystal's mom tried to explain it to her more than once. "It's not like they get as much exposure to us as we get to them," she said. "How many TV shows have white people in them? There are so many that we get to learn a lot about different kinds of white people. But the shows on TV that have people like us on them are very few, and they end up making us all sound and look alike. It's not their fault that they don't see it, but I do wish they'd be a little more curious."

Crystal had lots of time to think, and she loved being alone. She started keeping a diary, too, after getting one with a key for Christmas last year. That was tricky because she shared a bedroom with her younger sister, Trina, who was pretty nosy. But Crystal found the perfect hiding place for it, inside a cookie tin, up on the top shelf of the closet, where Trina couldn't reach it. Her favorite time to write in it was when Trina was watching TV downstairs.

October 10th

Tawana skipped out of lunch today and sneaked into town with the cool kids again. She didn't get caught this time, but I know it's gonna happen. I can't make her see the big chance she's taking. What if she gets caught? She's the only one with something to lose. She can get kicked out of school. The Gilmore kids can't. And then, what would happen to me? She's really my only friend in the whole damn place. I swear she never thinks ahead. I do. If I know about anything, it's about what might happen. Consequences — that's my specialty.

School isn't so hard. Life isn't so hard. You've just got to pay attention and do what you're told, and it'll all work out. At least it has so far.

Maybe I should start helping Tawana with her homework. But no! She doesn't want to learn how to do it. She just wants to copy mine. And I'll be damned if I'm gonna let her get caught cheating with my homework. Then I'll get a zero, too. All she cares about these days is Danny and Suzy and the other dumbass cool kids. Can't she see they're just losers?

I'm aiming to get on the honor roll this term. And all this year, too. I want to get the prize for the most conscientious student on our team. Mom says all those awards and things count when you apply for college. Mom's good about things like that. She knows I'm really trying to work hard, get ahead, and get a good education. It makes her happy to see me working so hard. And it's not so bad.

Crystal was starting to feel drowsy. She yawned and let out a high note as she exhaled. She put down her pen, locked up her diary, and put it back in its hiding place, stretching her entire five-foot-five to place it securely on the shelf in the closet. As she slid under the covers, she looked at her list of Beanie Babies, saw that the next name was Lenny the Lion, and picked it up out of the tub with all the others. Wanting to be fair to all of them, Crystal slept holding a different one each night, in order. Tonight was Lenny's turn.

Lenny had a soft yellow body, and his mane and tail were both made of dark-brown yarn. His face was sweet and friendly, like all the Beanie Babies. Crystal placed him carefully on her pillow then remembered her parents. She got back out of bed and ran downstairs to say goodnight.

It had been a tough day, but she felt better after writing in her diary.

Chapter Three

Five o'clock? Already? Crystal would never be a morning person. Most days, talking to Tawana was her first actual conversation of the day. Sometimes she couldn't even remember her feet climbing onto the bus, not that it was all that important. It was the same, day in and day out.

This morning was different, though. Tawana wasn't on the bus. So Crystal sat alone, staring out the window, watching the storefronts along Blue Hill Avenue, all with "CLOSED" signs in the door-ways. In some of them, Crystal could see a huddled figure, lying against the door, covered up with cardboard, or maybe a jacket. Her eyes gazed on them, but she didn't stare.

Some people didn't have a home to sleep in. It usually wasn't their fault, her dad had told her. He had lots of stories about people he knew who were going through hard times. One was kicked out of the mental hospital because his insurance ran out. He wasn't dangerous, but he couldn't get a job and find a place to live by himself. Another story was about the landlord who kicked whole families out of a building because he sold it to a developer who was trying to "rebuild Boston." Lots of people lost their homes along the way. That didn't make them bad people.

Crystal preferred to pass them by on the bus, though. It scared her to be close enough to street people to smell them. Why couldn't they clean themselves? She finally asked her father one day. He was sitting in the living room, listening to his favorite Frank Morgan jazz CD, and she could tell by the slow, deep breaths he was taking that it was a good time to talk. If you tried right when he came home, he might ignore you. Crystal's dad worked at Beth Israel Hospital as a unit secretary on the cardiac floor, so there were lots of emergencies happening all the time. It took a while for him to "let go of the day's details," as he liked to put it. Frank Morgan's saxophone helped him change channels from work to home.

"Dad, why do poor people have to smell so bad? I mean, don't they want to be clean? Don't they know any better?" she had asked.

Crystal's dad looked at his daughter and pulled her close to him. She could smell the Old Spice that he always wore. She knew he liked these conversations, liked to see that Crystal was thinking about the world and what made it tick.

"Poor people smell the way they do because baths and showers are the luxury of people who have a home with running water," he said. "Think about it. Even if they do manage to find a place with a shower, like the YMCA, for instance, if all they have to wear is what they're wearing, how are they going to get their clothes clean?"

She never thought of it that way. Crystal was just beginning to be curious about so many things that didn't seem fair. She wanted to grow up and do something about it, something important that would make a difference. She wasn't quite sure how yet, but somebody ought to do something, and it might as well be her.

These thoughts and many more flitted in and out of her head as the bus made its way out of the city and toward Gilmore. The traffic eased quite a bit, since most people were commuting to work and school the other way, toward the business centers of Boston. One of Crystal's favorite parts was when they crossed the Charles River, and she could see rowers making their way in their long, narrow boats.

She noticed athletic-looking people in their brightly colored workout clothes and matching sneakers, the women with bright-red lipstick. Who in their right mind, Crystal wondered, would put on makeup to go outdoors and work up a sweat? Women on the prowl, that's who, even at that hour of the day.

As the bus made its way up the hill to Gilmore, Crystal felt her stomach tighten the way it always did at this point. She braced herself for the day, not sure what it would bring, not even sure Tawana would show up without the bus to bring her.

But there she was, huddled in a corner with the cool kids. Crystal looked over at them, ready to say hi, but Tawana just looked away from her. Crystal looked down quickly. She wanted it to seem like she hadn't even noticed.

It made her angry, though. Who did Tawana think she was, ignoring her, someone who sat with her every darn day on the bus, who was her only real friend in this place?

She'd show Tawana what it felt like. All the way upstairs to homeroom, Crystal plotted her revenge. First, she would not look at her in any of their classes today. Then at lunch she'd go sit with someone else. Then, if Tawana came up to her and wanted to know what was wrong, Crystal would pretend nothing was the matter, just toss her head and walk away.

❋ ❋ ❋

But none of that happened, because Tawana didn't show up in any of her classes that morning. She never made it into the building. Neither did Danny or Suzanne. Where were they? What kind of trouble were they into now?

By lunchtime, Crystal couldn't stand not knowing. She sneaked out of the building and headed into Gilmore's town center. She knew the store they liked to hang out in, so that's where she went. As she got closer, she heard voices coming from behind a truck parked outside the grocery store. She heard giggling, and recognized Tawana.

"Tawana, I know you're over there," said Crystal.

Silence. More giggles.

"Crystal is that you? Come over here, quick before anyone sees you. There's a cop on the corner," said Tawana.

Crystal looked around quickly and felt a hand on her arm pulling her behind the truck. She looked up and saw Danny, Jamie, Travis and Suzanne crouching over Tawana who was eating chips out of a plastic bag and trying to write.

"Want some?" she offered her friend.

"What is that?" Crystal asked.

"Chips, what do you think?" Tawana said.

"No, I mean what are you writing?" Crystal asked.

"It's just a note."

Crystal craned her neck to read what was there. "But it says it's to Billy from Lee."

"Yeah, we're writing a note and sticking it in

Billy's locker. This is going to be great!" said Suzanne, a tall, thin girl with long dirty blond hair and a pair of jeans that looked like she painted them on.

"He's never going to know who did this," said Danny, whose thick brown hair fell into his eyes, making it hard to see the expression on his face.

"Why are you writing it, Tawana? And whose idea was this, anyway?" Crystal asked.

"I don't know," said Tawana. "It's just a joke."

"What's it say?" She pulled it out of Tawana's hands, and read it out loud. 'Billy, I think you're so cute, and you have a sweet little butt.' "What?" said Crystal.

"Give it back, Crystal. It's just a joke. Everyone knows Lee is gay, and we're just going to help things move along, that's all." Tawana's attempt to convince Crystal wasn't working.

"What do you mean, Lee is gay? Lee is from Thailand, for godsakes. He's only been in this country one year. Why are you picking on him?"

"Oh, Crystal, lighten up. We're only kidding with him," said Travis. Because he had an older brother on the soccer team, Travis was given a lot of slack at Gilmore, but he was not the clean-cut student his brother was. There was a time that Crystal even felt sorry for Travis because he was always being compared with his big brother, but not today.

"This is stupid. I can't believe you're doing this. I can't believe you're cutting school, too, Tawana. You're already in trouble, remember?"

"Look who's talking," said Danny. "Shouldn't you be on your way to class now, Crystal?"

"I'm only looking out for my friend, trying to keep her out of trouble," said Crystal. "Not that you care. But if she gets kicked out of Gilmore, well, let's just say I don't want that to happen, and if you were a real friend, you wouldn't be asking her to write stupid notes like this."

Jamie and Travis looked at each other then stepped forward. "Hey, nobody asked you to come along. Go back to school if that's what you want to do. Just leave Tawana alone. She can make her own decisions. Right, Tawana?" said Jamie.

"It's okay, Crystal, really," Tawana said. "Suzanne forged my mom's signature on an absentee note, so I'm covered for today. But you better hurry back. It's getting late."

Crystal looked at her watch and knew Tawana was right. She ran back to school, getting stitches in her side that slowed her down. Ms. Levantov, her English teacher, saw her coming in the front door.

"Where have you been, young lady?" she asked.

"I was just...my..." she stammered.

"Why don't you come with me and explain it to Mr. Davis? I've got a class, but he'll be very interested in your story, I'm sure." Mr. Davis was the assistant principal in charge of discipline. Of all the people Crystal did not want to see, he was at the top of her list.

"But I don't want to be late for social studies," Crystal said.

"This will only take a minute," said Ms. Levantov.

Crystal walked out five minutes later with a week's worth of detention. Great. Now she had two choices: either stay after once a week for five weeks on late bus day, or have to tell her mother and get it over with in one week. If she chose the second one, she'd have to take the public buses and trains home every day but one.

Crystal decided to do the once-a-week thing. Her mother and father didn't need to know she was in trouble. This way, she wouldn't have to tell them.

This was not fair. She was just trying to help her friend. Tawana wasn't even getting into trouble, and she was skipping the whole day. She hated that look Mr. Davis gave her, as if she were now a bad kid, doomed, her reputation ruined forever. She'd been working hard for years, always following the rules, and now, with one mistake, she was on the Bad Kid list. And there was her friend, about to start some real trouble, and she could do nothing to stop it.

Where were they now? Probably stealing more stuff from the small grocery store owned by an Armenian family in town. Danny said they charged too much anyway. He made it sound like ripping these people off was only fair. What a jerk. The thing that she couldn't stop thinking about was they were going to get away with skipping school for the whole day. For Danny and Suzanne, it wouldn't really matter. They lived in Gilmore. Nothing bad was going to happen to them. But Tawana had a lot to lose. Didn't she get it? She wasn't the same as them. How could she be so stupid?

That night, Crystal wrote in her diary:

October 20th

If I ever graduate from this school, it'll be a miracle. It's like I stand out worse than a sore thumb. It's more like I'm the only chocolate donut in the box, or the only burnt potato chip. People notice me. I wish they didn't. I wish I could be invisible most of the time. I wish they'd all just leave me alone.

But the problem was, a lot of them *did* leave her alone. She was invisible when people were picking partners for science projects or pals to study with or people to swap secrets with. Now, she was even invisible to Tawana. She didn't know how to deal with this.

Was she just being stupid, like Tawana said? Trying to play fair when she would never be treated fairly? Thinking that if she just obeyed all the rules, she could be happy and get ahead, too? What if, after trying really hard and staying out of trouble, she didn't end up any better off than Tawana? Was she missing all the fun of growing up? Because fun is exactly what was missing in her life these days.

She couldn't be wrong, could she? But what was so much fun about skipping school and getting kicked off the bus and having teachers talk about you when they ate lunch together in the faculty room?

But what if they already did? There were some teachers who didn't even see Crystal raising her hand to answer a question. Mr. James, the math teacher, was the worst one. She got so tired of waving her hand in the air and not getting called on, she stopped doing it. Let him think she didn't know the answer. What did she care?

But wasn't that just playing into his game? That way, Mr. James could say, 'These COMBOS kids just don't try. They don't have the intelligence of other Gilmore kids.' But it was humiliating never to be called on.

Chapter Four

Ms. Jones was good about this kind of thing. She had lunch with any COMBOS kids who wanted to have lunch with her once a week, and Crystal noticed how the seventh and eighth graders seemed to understand a kind of code with Ms. Jones. She wouldn't come right out and criticize a teacher, but she would listen. She wouldn't pounce on a kid for talking, either.

One time, Ms. Jones told Ms. Allen, the principal, about a new teacher who said something derogatory about Roxbury, a section of Boston lots of the COMBOS kids came from, and Ms. Allen called that new teacher down as soon as she was told about it.

Crystal heard all about it from Denisha, the student who had complained to Ms. Jones. "You actually got a teacher in trouble?" Crystal asked.

"Yeah. I heard her say something about Roxbury in class in a role-play situation, and she made it sound like Roxbury was the worst place on earth — uncivilized even."

"What did you do?"

"I told my Mom, and she got on the horn with Ms. Jones, and my mom was fit to be tied. I mean, I never heard her talk like that before, saying stuff like, 'I live in a very respectable neighborhood, and you know, we are part of a neighborhood association, and I'll be damned if this highfalutin new teacher, who has probably never even been to Roxbury, is going to make it sound like we live in a jungle. I've got a flower garden that some *Boston*

Globe photographer took pictures of and put in the magazine section a few Sundays ago. Nobody's going to run down my part of the city and get away with it. She has no right, no right.' Ms. Jones couldn't even get a word in edgewise." Denisha kept laughing at the memory.

"Well, what happened?"Crystal asked.

"Ms. Jones marched right into Ms. Allen's office, and the principal called the new teacher down right then and there, and the two of them asked her what her version of the story was. She admitted it! She said she was just into the role-play. That's not how she really thinks, and blah, blah, blah, and you know what? The principal said she'd better take that course on racism and stereotypes next time they offered it, the very next semester. Ms. Jones said it was a sweet moment."

"I wonder if she could do anything about Mr. James," said Crystal. "That man just won't call on me. I can have my hand up in his face for 45 minutes straight, and he won't ever call on me. He don't even see me."

"Doesn't," Denisha corrected.

"You knew what I meant," said Crystal.

"Yes, but if you don't talk right and white around here, people assume you're not very smart. I finally learned that lesson the hard way."

Crystal looked up to Denisha. She was going into the high school next year, and she had been on the honor roll every term. Denisha was bright and funny and kind, and Crystal wanted to be just like her. "You know, sometimes I just don't wanna talk white. It's not that I can't. It's just...limiting, you know? I can't really express my feelings the same way."

"I understand. But Mr. James? He's beyond help. He's not going to change — not for anything. And he's been here so long, the union will back him up no matter what he does. That new teacher, she really didn't mean any harm. She actually apologized to me."

"Well, that's something," said Crystal.

"It's better than what I'm used to around here. Most of the time, if you complain, they just talk about how you misunderstood them," said Denisha.

"I've been black my whole life," said Crystal. "If there's one thing I understand pretty well, it's racism. I've had first-hand experience with that."

"I hear you."

"Denisha, are you glad you're going to Gilmore High School next year?" Crystal asked.

"I don't know. I guess, because they've got a diversity club going there, and I think I can play basketball and field hockey. I"m pretty good, even if I'm just starting out."

"I hate being one of the only black people. Do you ever get used to it?"

"Yeah, I'm used to it. That's not the same as liking it, though. Hey, where's Tawana been?"

"Don't even go there," said Crystal.

"Why? What's up?"

"She's hanging around with Danny and Suzanne, and getting into trouble, or just barely staying out of trouble."

Denisha rolled her eyes and shook her head. "Is she crazy?"

"I think so, but Tawana is just sick of school and figures that if she can hang with those kids, and they like her, she'll have more fun here. Personally, I think it's gonna backfire on her, though."

"I'm gonna have to have a talk with that girl," said Denisha.

"I wish someone could talk some sense into her. I've tried but she won't listen to me anymore."

Ms. Jones walked in on the tail end of their discussion. "Who's in trouble?"

"You know who," said Crystal. "We're talking about Tawana. But I really want to talk about Mr. James. Is he allowed to ignore one of his students through an entire class, day after day?"

"Would this student be you, Crystal?"

"Well, maybe. Yes, actually it is. I raise my hand every darn day, and he never calls on me, not once!"

"Well, maybe that's because he knows you know the answer."

"Isn't that why we raise our hands?" said Crystal. "Is there something here I'm not getting?"

"If he knows you know, maybe he's the kind of teacher who registers that, and then calls on someone who might not know," said Ms. Jones.

"Teachers are a strange breed," said Crystal. "I think he doesn't call on me because I'm black."

"Well, does he call on Tawana? Or Derek?" Ms. Jones asked.

"Yes."

"Well, there goes that theory," said Ms. Jones.

"But they never do their homework, so they don't know what they're doing! They just sit there acting stupid."

"Just goes to prove my point," said Ms. Jones.

"But then he calls on a white kid with her hand up, and it's always a white kid who gives the right answer. I can't prove it, Ms. Jones, but I just know he's racist."

"I'm not arguing with your experience, Crystal. I'm not in that class, so I don't know what goes on, and I trust you're telling me the truth. I'm just saying that teachers don't often act the way their students want them to, regardless of their color."

"Yeah, maybe," said Crystal.

"He did the same with me," said Denisha.

"You know, we've got to choose our battles here," Ms. Jones said.

Crystal looked hard at Ms. Jones, her mouth set, grim and determined. "What's that supposed to mean, Ms. Jones? Am I supposed to just sit there in that class and vegetate, pretend I don't know what I know, and never get credit for what I do know? Because that's just unfair—and don't go telling me life isn't fair. I already know that."

"Crystal, does Mr. James give tests and quizzes?" asked Ms. Jones.

"Tests, but no quizzes."

"Do you hand in your homework every day?"

"Yes."

Ms. Jones looked at Crystal as if her point had just been proven again.

Denisha let out a deep sigh and faced the seventh grader one more time, eyeball to eyeball. "Just keep your nose clean, Crystal, and don't give him anything to punish you for. If you keep doing your work, he's got to give you a good grade in math."

"What if he doesn't give me an A because I don't participate in class? Some teachers do that," said Crystal. She was in tears now, tears of frustration, and they were spilling down her cheeks. "It's just the way he is that makes me so angry," she said. "And I sit there in that class with all that anger, and it gets in the way of my hearing anything he tries to say. He's so condescending, it makes me want to punch him out."

Lots of times, the lunches with Ms. Jones were just like this, gripe sessions. It didn't change much, but it was a good way to let off some steam. Crystal liked Denisha and wished they lived closer, or better yet, were in the same grade.

When she got home that night, Crystal brought it up with her mom. When she was finished, her mom put her arm around Crystal and pulled her close.

"Crystal, how many times do I have to tell you," said her mom, "this is just racial nonsense. It can happen anywhere, and probably will happen everywhere you go. It's just the way things are. If you can do well at Gilmore, you'll have an excellent foundation. That means you can do well anywhere, no matter who's in charge. I want you to have all the chances in the world. And there's no reason for you not to succeed. You're bright, you work hard—"

"I know, but I could be doing so much better, Mom. I just know I could. I wish I didn't feel like I had to fight this all the time. It's right here in my throat, and I can't breathe sometimes."

"Try not to think about this right now, Crystal. It's been a long day. You're tired, you've got homework to do, and I could use some help cleaning up this kitchen."

Crystal sighed and pitched in. She always pitched in. She liked this time with her mom. They put on a good CD, Stevie Wonder's *Songs in the Key of Life,* and the two of them sang and danced till everything was done and the kitchen was sparkling again. Crystal and her mother would sometimes trade solos, and then hoot and holler if one of them sang in perfect timing with Stevie's "If It's Magic."

> *It holds the key to every heart*
> *Throughout the universe...*

All too soon, the kitchen chores were done, and Crystal had to get down to her homework. She didn't have to be pushed to do that, though. And tonight, even math seemed easier to her.

When she kissed her mom and dad good night, her dad asked her, seriously, "Do you want me to call Ms. Jones and talk about this math teacher, Princess? I can do that, you know. I'm not sure what good it would do, and my getting involved just might make things worse, but I'll do it if you think it would help."

"Thanks, Dad. I'll let you know. Mom's probably right."

"You're *my* princess, that's who you are," her dad said, squeezing her tightly. "And don't you ever forget it."

Crystal rolled her eyes, but she was smiling on the inside.

Before she went to bed, she unlocked her diary and took the cap off her favorite pen.

October 21st

Dad called me his princess tonight. He hasn't done that in a while.

I think I'm a little spoiled, expecting people at Gilmore who hardly know me at all to treat me the way Mom, Dad, Gram, and even the choirmaster at church do. Around here, I'm somebody. At Gilmore, I don't like the somebody they think I am. And so I go around wanting to be a nobody. And that's what's tearing me up inside. The pastor was saying just last week, "Don't go hiding your light under a bushel basket."

I've got to get used to dealing with people like Mr. James. Not everybody's gonna want to see me shine, but that doesn't mean I won't or I don't. I just have to be careful and remember what I'm there for — a better education, a better future, and more opportunities.

Chapter Five

Thursday morning, Crystal was approached by Ms. Levantov before walking into homeroom. She didn't know what to expect. The last time Crystal had been approached by her, she'd bagged her for going out of the building during lunchtime. This time, she looked as though she didn't even remember that incident. "Crystal," Ms. Levantov said, "I need your help."

"Yes, Ma'am?"

"I am really worried about Derek and Tawana this term. They're falling way behind, and I was hoping you'd be wiling to help me tutor them."

"Me? Tutor other seventh graders?" she asked.

"Well, if you wouldn't mind. I just know how easy English is for you, especially the reading and journal-response writing we're doing. I thought it would be good to just have a few minutes at the end of class where you three could go into the workshop area and get started on the homework. What do you think?"

Crystal panicked. She could feel her intestines tie themselves into a knot as she realized what Ms. Levantov was asking her to do. The last thing she wanted was to shove her intelligence in Tawana's face. Yes, English came easily to Crystal because she liked to read, and the words made sense to her. But Tawana hated this class, and the two of them weren't exactly getting along these days.

What made Ms. Levantov think she could help Tawana? She was the teacher. Crystal was just another student. What she wanted to say was,

"Look, Ms. Levantov, the only help Tawana ever wants from me is permission to copy my homework. This is just not going to work." But of course she couldn't say that.

"Sure, I'll try," Crystal said. How could she say no?

"Thank you so much," Ms. Levantov said. "We'll start today."

Great. Crystal felt a couple of sharp pangs in her belly. She noticed it more these days since she and Tawana had drifted apart. Before, just a look across the room when one of them was having a problem communicating with someone at Gilmore, and the pain would go away. But today, she knew it was just going to get worse.

When Tawana walked into homeroom, Crystal was already sitting there. Tawana didn't even look at her. They sat pretty close to each other, in assigned seats, and Tawana was giggling with Suzanne about something. Crystal wondered whatever happened to the note she saw. Maybe they had decided not to plant it in Billy's locker. She didn't dare ask Tawana, though. Her thoughts were flying around in her head so fast she didn't even hear the announcements. The only way she knew they were over was everyone was getting up and moving around.

"Did you do the English?" Tawana asked Crystal, not even making eye contact.

"Yes, you know I did," said Crystal.

"Ms. Levantov gave me a warning slip. I think she mailed it home to my mother. I'm failing that class, too."

"Well, she asked me if I would help tutor you and Derek. Seems like you both need help in English."

"Who did what?" asked Derek, hearing his name as he walked behind them out into the hall.

"Ms. Levantov asked me to help you guys get started on your homework, you know, help explain things."

"What, because you know how us dumb black kids would be thinking, and you could set us straight?" said Derek, his tone angry and insulted.

"Well, she's giving you the benefit of the doubt that the reason you're not doing it is you don't understand it. It's more than I would do for your sorry-ass laziness," said Crystal.

"I don't need your help. Wouldn't mind getting some help from a real teacher, though," said Tawana.

"Hey, I didn't ask for this. How could I say no?"

"You coulda just told her the truth, that you're not a teacher, and you don't have the slightest idea how to help us," said Tawana.

"Won't that look just peachy," said Derek. "The three black kids huddled together trying to understand the big bad homework assignment that all the white kids are just skipping home to do by themselves."

"Don't blame me! Tell her yourself! I just wanted you to know what to expect in class today."

"Today? She's starting this tutoring today?" said Tawana.

"Why did I even open my mouth?" muttered Crystal. "I should've known you two would take it like this. How do you think I feel? I'd rather start my own homework, thank you very much. It's not like you two ever listen to me, anyway."

"This is stupid and embarrassing," said Tawana. "I know. I'm gonna get a pass from Ms. Jones for that whole class."

"See if you can get one for me, too," said Derek.

"You know what?" Crystal said through clenched teeth. "I don't care what you do. Flunk this class. See if I care. I don't need this aggravation." Crystal turned her back and walked away from those people she used to call her friends.

On her way to another class, Crystal made a stop at Ms. Jones' office. "Can I talk to you?"

"Right now? Don't you have a class to go to?" Ms. Jones asked.

"I'm on my way to the gym, but something is really bothering me."

"Okay, Crystal. What's the problem?"

"It's English. Ms. Levantov has this bright idea for me to start tutoring Derek and Tawana, right in class, in front of everybody, at the last few minutes of the period to help them get started on their homework. Ms. Jones, they're not gonna listen to me. I just told them about it now so they wouldn't be caught off guard, and they're gonna ask you for a pass. We COMBOS kids gotta stick together. I know that. But this isn't the way. I mean, it's crazy, but I feel disloyal doing this. And how's it gonna look to everybody else in the class? I mean, the three of us already stand out like sore thumbs."

"I see your point. I'll try to talk to Ms. Levantov before your class. What time do you meet today?"

"Eleven fifteen. Right before lunch. Do you think you could? I mean, I know she means well and everything, but..."

"I'll do my best. Thanks for telling me, Crystal."

Crystal felt a little better walking out of there,

but she knew it wasn't a done deal. Just because you could see trouble coming didn't mean it didn't come. A commotion in the hallway had kids flying out of the gym when it was clearly not time for that kind of hubbub.

"What's going on?" Crystal asked the first person she recognized.

"Billy and Lee got into a fight," the boy said. "It started in the locker room, but Billy went after Lee just now, in the middle of volleyball. He's smaller than Lee, but boy was he mad. Started calling him a faggot and telling him to leave him the hell alone!"

"Lee's mouth is bloody and he's crying," said another.

Uh oh. She knew exactly what this was all about. Tawana and Crystal were not in the same gym class, but she knew it was just a question of time. So this is what happened with that note business.

Crystal walked into the gym, and saw the gym teacher, Ms. Farling, tending to Lee's split lip. The other kids were huddled around Billy, trying to calm him down. Before another word was said, Mr. Davis came crashing through the double doors to the gym. "Billy? Can I have a word with you, please?"

Three of the boys standing with Billy said reassuring things to him. "You just tell him what happened," one of them said.

"Lee started it," another told Mr. Davis.

"You didn't do anything wrong, Billy," said a third boy.

"Just defending himself, Mr. Davis," the first one said.

"Thank you, boys, for your opinions. I'll take it from here." Billy looked pretty short and scrawny walking next to Mr. Davis, who was easily six feet tall and had played football in college. Now with his belly hanging over his belt buckle, he was definitely a big man.

Nothing Ms. Farling did could stop the whispers and the play-by-play descriptions of those few minutes in the locker room. She said, in her booming gym-teacher voice, "This was a pretty exciting way to start class, but people, we're going to play some volleyball now. Pay attention, will you? Someone's going to get hurt if you keep replaying that scuffle. Now focus!"

Crystal knew that Lee was not prepared for this. Nothing in Thailand could have prepared him for America's brand of homophobia. If you didn't like something, you said it was "gay." If you didn't like someone, you called him or her a "faggot." It wasn't an accurate word, usually. It was just another way to say "stupid" or "ugly" or "jerk."

But this note was different. People were looking at Lee as if he were really gay, as if what the note said was real. Crystal didn't understand why he was crying. Why didn't Lee fight back and deny the whole thing? He just caved in, collapsed. In her eyes, he couldn't have handled it worse.

Crystal dreaded English class, the last class of the day. Dreaded seeing her so-called friends. Derek and Tawana came in late. When they looked at Crystal, she could see they were mad.

"What's the problem here?" asked Ms. Levantov. "You're a good ten minutes late."

Tawana pursed her lips and looked right at Crystal. "We tried to make an appointment with Ms. Jones, but she was busy."

Ms. Levantov pursed her lips and looked directly at the two latecomers. "Ms. Jones spoke with me at lunchtime. I think I know what this is about," she said. "Well, all you missed was our going over last night's homework assignment. Do you have something to give me?"

"No, Ma'am," said Tawana, with no trace of apology in her voice.

"I think mine's in my locker," said Derek. Ms. Levantov shook her head and tsked loud enough for everyone to hear, not at all convinced.

If looks could kill, Crystal would have been bleeding from a head wound. What was Tawana's problem? She was used to being misunderstood by everyone else in that room, but not by Tawana.

At the end of class, Ms. Levantov whispered to Crystal, "Let's talk about this some more tomorrow during homeroom, okay?"

Why was she doing this, Crystal wondered, acting like they were cooking up this scheme together, just the two of them?

"Okay, sure," said Crystal. "Whatever," she muttered under her breath.

Chapter Six

Crystal couldn't wait to see Tawana in the safety zone of the COMBOS bus. "Okay, so who did it? Who actually put the note in Billy's locker? Was it you? I hope it wasn't you because that would be just about the stupidest setup the world has ever seen."

Tawana just stared at her, saying nothing.

"You did it, didn't you? You fell for their lies, the little carrot on the stick. Did they promise to be your friends forever? Did they start inviting you to their parties? Huh? Well, don't just sit there, Tawana. Tell me the truth."

"I'm not saying nothin' to you. I got nothin' to say."

"Well if you didn't do it, I wish you'd ease my mind. Don't you think you owe me that as your friend, your only real friend in this school?"

Tawana stared at Crystal for a good long moment. Her face was filling up with emotion, Crystal could see, and mostly it looked like anger.

"Some friend you are. You act all high and mighty, better than everyone. You get points for being our tutor, when you wouldn't help me with my homework when I asked you to, like a real friend would."

"What? When did you ever ask for my help with homework? And wanting to copy it from me doesn't count," she added quickly.

"Stop acting like this is about homework or school at all, because it's not. This is about me making friends with kids that don't ride on this bus, and I think you're just jealous," said Tawana.

"Jealous? Of Dizzy Suzy and Drippy Danny? I

don't think so. If you don't see that they're just using you, just cozying up to their new black buddy so they can look all hip and cool and get you to do the things they don't want to get in trouble for, well then you're dumber than I thought."

"That's cold, Crystal. If you don't want to be friends with them, that's your business. But you can't stop me from making friends, you know. And who said we have to be best friends, anyway? People change. I'm changing. I don't want to be Miss Smarty-Pants-Know-It-All. I want to be me. And have a little fun. And you are getting to be a real drag."

Crystal stepped back as if she'd been slapped. Nothing Tawana said could have hurt more than this. Crystal was afraid she was turning into some kind of homework machine, all work and no play. She didn't see a way around it, though. And now, here was Tawana telling her exactly what she'd been feeling for a while now, that Tawana wasn't her friend, either.

"Tawana, you know I gotta do this or my parents will kill me. My mother, especially. She's got her heart set on me going to some really good college, probably because she missed her chance."

"Do you hear yourself? Crystal, you're thirteen, not eighteen. Why are you worried about college already?"

"Cause the only way I'm gonna get to college is to make an impression here, right here, at Gilmore Middle School and then, when I get to high school, do the same thing there. Look how many people we know, really smart people, and they're just hanging on the corner. We see them every day on our way home. I don't want to end up like that, Tawana. I want to make something of myself. Don't you?"

"Well, yeah, but I don't think I'm goin' to college, Crystal. I think maybe I'll get my hairdresser's license and work in the beauty shop with my cousin. I think I'd like that. You don't have to go to college for that. I'm not stupid but I hate school.

Hate it, hate it, hate it. And being around you makes me realize what it takes to get good grades, and I just don't want to do it. It's a choice I'm making."

"Tawana, do you really think you'll be happy cutting hair the rest of your life?"

"I don't know, but I sure don't want to go to school for eight more years. Who knows? Maybe I'll get married and work part time, something like that."

The two girls sat back in their seats, not another word said between them. The bus fumes were getting to Crystal, the way they always did the closer she got to her neighborhood. Outside, the sun was slicing through the shady trees near Franklin Park, and she could see emaciated men of who-knows-what age leaning against the street signs at the entrance to the park.

Crystal loved Franklin Park. She enjoyed Sundays there with her family. After church, they would bring some food and have a picnic, firing up a grill and eating some ribs, or some barbecued chicken, with corn on the cob plastered with butter and sprinkled with salt, so sweet it would make you smile, the kernels sticking between your teeth and you didn't even care who saw it.

Her favorite time was the Kite Festival in May, when everyone in Boston would show up to fly a kite. There were so many flying so high, it looked like confetti in the sky. That was a day even white people came back to Franklin Park every year. It was the only time you saw a mix of people there. Most of the time, whites didn't even want to drive through it, on Columbus Avenue, even though it was the fastest way to get from Jamaica Plain to Dorchester. Too dangerous.

Lots of golfers were out this afternoon, and plenty of joggers, too. Crystal felt proud. What would Gilmore kids think if they ever ventured here? They might be surprised to see black people with a set of golf clubs, playing in a park this green and spacious they could call their own.

It was strange, the thoughts that would spin around in her head as she drove back and forth between city and suburb. On the one hand, Gilmore kids took everything for granted. Their families drove big cars to get anywhere at all, even if the bus or subway could get them there just as easily. Their supermarkets had the best produce. Their homes had a television set in every bedroom, a smaller one in the kitchen, and a huge one in the living room. The Blaines even had a computer in every bedroom. They fed their dog the same food they ate for dinner. Crystal couldn't get over that. Imagine the dog eating his own pork chop. In Crystal's world, that would be wasteful. Bones, sure. Scraps, of course. But a whole serving? Never.

On the other hand, Crystal's family was not poor. In her neighborhood, they were considered "comfortable." Crystal's dad had a good job working for the hospital, and they were highly respected in their church. When the kids from the suburbs thought of Dorchester, which was hardly ever, all they had were scenes from movies or the local TV news — drive-by shootings, drugs, and graffiti everywhere. Not that Crystal didn't know about those things, but they were not part of her immediate, everyday world. Other people did them.

She knew better than to get involved in anything dangerous. She never went anywhere at night without her parents, for example. She didn't hang out with kids on the corners, so she wasn't exposed to what Gilmore kids thought of as street life anymore than they were.

She loved her big old house, with the wood accents everywhere, the built-in hutch in the dining room filled with her mother's best china, crystal glasses, and family photos. She loved her side of the bedroom that she shared with Trina. Okay, so it wasn't all that big, but she had a shelf lining the wall, and every inch of it was covered with her Beanie Babies. She counted forty-five of them just the other day, and she knew their names by heart.

Crystal was excited the first — and only — time Judy Blaine ever came to her house to play on a Saturday, back in third grade, when they first met. She couldn't wait to show her that collection. Judy was pretty impressed. She had her own Beanie Baby collection, and they had a lot of the same ones. Having that in common helped a lot, but Crystal couldn't ignore how different their lives really were once she'd seen where Judy lived.

Judy lived on a tree-lined street, and her house had a half-acre of land around it. There was a wooden swing set for her and her brother but a full-sized trampoline just for Judy. Every person in that family had their own room, even Judy's parents. The bed was in the master bedroom, but each of them also had their own office space where they spent time reading, talking on the phone, whatever. So much room for four people. And Judy's grandmother had her own apartment over the three-car garage.

When Crystal finally came home after that visit, she felt ashamed of where she lived for the first but not the last time. She noticed things, like the cracks in the paint in the hallway and the dust bunnies on the stairs, the seams that didn't quite meet in the wallpaper in the dining room, and the scuffed-up wood on doors, frames, and banisters. In Crystal's neighborhood, owning your own home was rare. That put them in the "well-off category" here. But after seeing Judy's house, that didn't seem like such a big deal anymore.

Still, she was glad that she had family members on every floor, that someone was always home, that voices here didn't echo as they did at the Blaine residence. Crystal thought she would be lonely if she lived in the Blaine's house, but what lingered in her mind was how everything shone, from stainless steel in the kitchen to wood tables and furniture. Everything glistened.

✳ ✳ ✳

One Saturday morning, Crystal was helping her mom clean house.

"Mom, why doesn't our toilet ever get clean?" she asked. "I've been scrubbing the same spot with cleanser, over and over, and I know it's clean, but it just doesn't look clean."

"This is an old house with old plumbing, Crystal," said her mom. "I know it's clean. Those are just stains on the porcelain. I'm just grateful it works when we flush it."

"Yeah, but I sure wish I could see some results from all this elbow grease. Maybe we're using the wrong cleaner."

"What's all this interest you have in what the bathroom looks like? You never cared before."

"It's just that in Judy's house, everything always looks brand new."

"That's because it probably is." Crystal's mom looked at her daughter a little closer. "You've got nothing to be ashamed of, you know."

"I didn't say I was ashamed, Mom, I'm just asking…"

"Your father and I work very hard to keep this house up. I'm proud of our home, and I want you to be, too. Don't forget who you are, Crystal, That's not what we're sending you to that country-club school for."

Crystal heard the hurt in her mom's voice. "I know, Mom. I'm sorry. I didn't mean anything by it." Crystal was worried. She wasn't used to upsetting her mother this way. But she couldn't help thinking about how nice everything was for Judy Blaine. What if she had been born white, in a house like that? What if she always felt like she belonged in Gilmore, Massachusetts? It was too big a stretch. She couldn't imagine it.

Sometimes, the ideas in Crystal's head seemed to take shape, to have a life of their own. Lately, she found it harder and harder to know where those thoughts belonged. Talking about how she felt was a problem, but she could not keep it all in, either.

And worst of all, sometimes she didn't even want to try. It was like an idea would come, and it would be as big as a baseball. A little while later, it had grown to the size of a volleyball, and then a basketball, and then it was going to come out no matter what she did, no matter who was listening. She didn't want it to hurt anyone on the way out of her mouth, but it wasn't like she could control it, either. Afterward, she felt a little better, some relief that it was outside and not inside her anymore. But now, looking at her mother, she wished she'd said it in a different way. The last person in the world Crystal wanted to hurt was her mother. They needed each other. But Crystal needed to find a way to let things out, or she would explode.

That night, Crystal wrote in her diary, which she had started calling her journal:

October 24th

I wonder what Mom would do in this situation. Would she tell on Tawana, or tell someone what really happened, who was really responsible? I wish I could talk to her about it. It's too big a secret, but it's not my secret. Maybe if Mom knew, she'd tell Tawana's mother about it. I know Mom will be mad if she finds out I knew about it, but that might not ever happen. What a mess. I better just keep my mouth shut and hope it all blows over.

Chapter Seven

The next day, Crystal noticed that Lee was sitting alone at lunch. Billy had been suspended for hitting Lee. He got two days in the office with Mr. Davis. Crystal felt bad for Lee. She wished she could do something, but what? She thought about telling Mr. Davis who was responsible for the note but decided against it. Getting Tawana and the rest of them in trouble wouldn't really change things for Lee. That damage was already done. Billy, who was already a popular kid, was even more of a hero now, but Crystal doubted that Lee would ever get over this.

She looked over at the COMBOS kids' table, and decided not to go there. Tawana was sitting with her new friends on the opposite end of the cafeteria. Crystal walked slowly through the lunch line and took a deep breath before standing at the table in front of Lee.

"This seat saved?" she asked him.

He looked up quickly, startled at being approached by anyone but his regular lunch partner, Phong. "No," he said. "Phong is absent today."

Crystal sat down and noticed Lee's hands shaking as he ate his homemade lunch out of a plastic container. "What are you eating?" she asked.

"Sushi and rice," he said.

"Sushi, that's raw fish, right?"

"Yes," he said, looking down, not meeting her gaze.

"My mom likes it a lot, but I'm too chicken to try it."

Lee glanced carefully at her face, saw she wasn't

making fun of him, and smiled shyly at her. "It's really good," he said. "Try some?"

"No, I don't think so," she said. "I'll stick with pizza today."

It was not normal for one girl to sit with one boy at lunchtime, even if they were a couple. Crystal could feel some eyes on them, but she didn't care. The poor kid only had one friend, just like her, and he was not in school today, on the day Lee needed him most. Maybe that wasn't even a coincidence.

They ate for a minute or two in silence. Finally Crystal opened her mouth and hoped what came out didn't sound stupid.

"I think it was really mean, what happened yesterday," she said.

"Yes, thank you," he nodded to her, looking down at his plate.

"No, I mean it. Nobody deserves to be treated like that. It was a rotten thing to do, and you haven't even been here in this country more than a year. Even if someone meant it as a practical joke, it wasn't funny."

Lee looked at her again, and she could swear his eyes were filling up with tears.

"Now, I know this place," Crystal said. "It can be cold, but people usually forget things pretty quickly. That's because most people here are not all that smart and don't have much in the way of memory. As bad as it feels today, it probably won't feel this bad ever again. And not everyone is on Billy's side. I just wanted you to know."

"Thank you. Your name is Christine, yes?"

"No, I'm Crystal. We're in the same math class."

"Oh, yes, Crystal, I'm sorry. My English is not very good."

"Sounds fine to me," she said. "Well, I'm gonna move over to my regular table, but it just didn't seem right to have you sitting all by yourself all through lunch today. I don't know you very well, but I know when someone is treated badly, and you definitely were."

Was that Lee's lip, quivering? She better get out of there now. The last thing either one of them needed was more crying.

"See you in math class," she said.

"Yes, see you there," he said.

Later that evening, Crystal wrote in her journal:

October 25th

It felt good going up to Lee at lunch today. Nothing lonelier than sitting at lunch by yourself, the longest 23 minutes ever. I think he was pretty brave to come back to school the very next day after being humiliated. He could've stayed home and avoided people staring at him and whispering, but he didn't.

That was a beginning. Whenever Crystal saw Lee from that time on, they said hi to each other. It didn't solve Lee's problems, but it made Crystal feel better to help someone with bigger problems, at least in school.

Crystal and Lee started talking a bit in math class, whenever they were there a minute early. Crystal learned that Lee's father worked at Harvard, and his parents were going to find him a woman who lived in Thailand to marry when he was finished with college. He didn't even sound like he thought that was a strange idea.

After they'd known each other a while, Crystal asked him the question she'd had ever since that horrible day. "Lee, why didn't you hit him back? You could have creamed him. He's a lot smaller than you. Don't you know how to fight?"

"We don't believe in fighting in my family," Lee said. "If you hit someone after they hit you, they will hit you harder, then you will have to hit them harder, and both people can get hurt very badly. This way, Billy got his anger out, and that was the end of it."

"But the kids were calling you names and saying

you were too scared to do anything about it. Don't you care what people think of you?" she asked.

"People here at Gilmore, they don't like me now. If I had beaten Billy up, they would hate me more. They love Billy. I'm the outsider here." He sighed and went on. "I wish I had not started to cry. That I do regret, but he punched me in the mouth, and the tears just came. I could not stop them."

"But now they feel sorry for you. They don't know you are stronger than he is. Don't you care what they're saying about you?"

Lee looked at Crystal and then looked away. "Perhaps you know what it is like to have people judge you without knowing who you really are. I think sometimes we have this in common, Crystal." His eyes were warm and kind when they met hers.

She wanted to come back with some smart comment, but she couldn't think of one. She wanted it not to be true, to feel somehow better than he was because she had been born here in

America, because English was her native language, because she could choose her own husband, but she said nothing. Lee was telling her a truth that she didn't want to accept; but somehow, when he said it, it didn't seem so bad.

After that conversation, they sought out each other's company. Crystal quickly knew his schedule. She knew when he had social studies and when he came to school. She looked forward to math class every day. She wished she sat behind him so she could look at him more during the class, but she was in the same row, three seats ahead of him, and had to turn around to see him.

"Do you like Mr. James?" she asked him one day as they were leaving math class.

"I think he's a boring teacher, but he's nice to me."

"I think he's a racist. He never calls on me. Have you noticed that?"

"I don't see you raising your hand, so...no, Crystal."

"Well, I used to, but he never called on me, and I got tired of trying, I guess."

"I don't raise my hand, because I'm shy with my English," he told her.

"Well, you gotta get over that, Lee. There's nothing wrong with your English. Heck, you talk better than half the kids in this building who were born in the USA."

Lee smiled at this and held the door open for her as they walked into the stairwell. Out of the corner of her eye, Crystal saw Derek and Danny laughing at them. She closed her eyes and tossed her head, focusing all of her attention on Lee.

"Don't pay any attention to them, Lee," she said. "They're morons, and they'll always be morons."

On the way home that day, Derek couldn't wait to start in. He held his fist in front of his mouth as a makeshift microphone. "Crystal's got a gay lover! But will she ever win her true love? No, because Lee's heart is sworn to Billy!"

"Shut *up,* Derek. You sound like such a fool," said Crystal.

"Well, everyone knows you like him, and everyone knows he's a faggot, so I guess you're gonna get your first case of heartache, honey," said Derek, loud enough for everyone three rows up and back to hear.

"I hate you, Derek. I just hate you. I didn't want to hate you, because you know, there just aren't that many of us, and I try to put our differences aside, but you don't know what you're talking about here."

"I know flirting when I see it, Crystal, and you are batting those eyelashes a mile a minute at Mr. Fu Manchu, and I'm not the only one who sees it."

"I like Lee. I won't deny it. He and I are friends, and I like him a lot. He sure treats me with more respect than anyone on this bus does," she said.

"Crystal's with Lee, ridin' on his knee," Derek started in a sing-song voice.

"If you don't shut up right now, I'm going to throw something at you, and it won't be my empty lunch bag," she said.

"I think it's kinda sweet, two oddballs, freaks, not quite nerds, but almost...finding true love...but it's a sad story because Lee is in love with Billy, and..." continued Derek.

"I hate you, Derek, hate you with every bone in my body." She saw Tawana out of the corner of her eye, watching the scene but not getting involved. Tawana was ignoring her completely, even on the bus these days. This was one of those times when it would have been nice to have her friend sticking up for her. It hurt, but what could Crystal do?

Crystal opened up her backpack and pulled out a book to read, *The Color Purple,* by Alice Walker. It wasn't an assigned book but one of her mom's, and even though there was some R-rated stuff in it, Crystal's mother thought Crystal would get a lot out of it.

"Your mother lets you read that?" the girl sitting next to her said. "That's not a book for kids!"

"Well, I guess my mom knows I'm mature enough to handle it. Plus, I get tired of baby books and those teenybopper books. They're so boring."

Crystal soon got lost in her book. She forgot all about Derek, put him right out of her mind. But his words did haunt her for a while. What if Lee really were gay? He was nice to Crystal, as polite as could be, but he never did anything to make her think he liked her as a girlfriend. That was fine with Crystal, but she did wonder.

In health class that year, they had learned all about sexual orientation. Her teacher, Ms. Devin, had explained that it was about attraction—you were attracted to certain people or you weren't. You couldn't make yourself like someone just because someone told you it would be a good idea. And whether you were heterosexual or homosexual, you didn't automatically like everyone of a certain gender. People are particular about who they like.

Crystal wanted to know if what people were saying about Lee was true. She didn't want to judge him for it. She was just interested. Could she ask him something that personal? It was hard to know how to bring it up, even.

Chapter Eight

The next time she and Lee had a chance to talk was lunch the next day. Crystal and he had been eating lunch at the same table with Phong for a few days now. Munching on carrots, chips and choco-late-chip cookies, Crystal and Lee talked about Mr. James and Ms. Jones and all kinds of things. Crystal noticed they both would put their hands shyly over their mouths if they were trying to say something and still chewing. She thought that was funny.

Suddenly, Tony, a large-sized seventh-grade boy, came crashing into their end of the lunch table, spilling their drinks. Crystal jumped up and wiped the table off with extra napkins.

"Tony! Watch where you're going! Look at yourself—you've got food all over you!" yelled Crystal.

"He pushed me!" Tony was laughing as he pointed at Danny. "Don't blame me. I couldn't help it."

Crystal wanted to hit Danny good and hard. She looked over at Lee who was still sitting down, red-faced with shame. Crystal sat back down and stared at Lee until he looked her in the eye.

"Lee, you can't let them keep doing this to you," she said.

"What am I supposed to do? I cannot stop them from these things," Lee said.

"Well, you can't just let them walk all over you. Did you ever try yelling at them? Or pushing back?"

"What good would that do? I don't want to cause a scene. I just want them to go away and leave me alone," he said.

"You're making it too easy for them to pick on you. That's what I think," said Crystal. "They don't understand things like dignity and honor. This is a war zone, Lee, and you've got to show them what you're made of."

"I am," he said.

"No, I don't believe it. You're not a sniveling little victim."

"You're different, Crystal. You're...what's the word...feesty?"

"Feisty," she corrected.

"That's right, feisty. You don't take abuse from anyone. I see you all the time, standing up for yourself. But I'm not like that. I'm from Thailand. We don't yell. Besides, I wouldn't know what to say. My English is not so good."

"Now don't go starting that bad-English stuff. I understand you perfectly. Everyone here does."

"I'm sorry, Crystal. I know you are trying to help me. I'm hopeless."

Crystal could see they were at a crossroads here. Maybe even a stalemate. But she had to keep trying. Danny was a bully, and Crystal didn't believe that bullies should be allowed to rule. It went against every belief she had in basic fairness. "Lee," she asked, "Can I ask you something? Is it true what they say about you liking Billy?"

Lee looked down at his feet quickly, then up again in Crystal's eyes. A wave of defiance crossed his once-passive face. "Yes, I do," he said. "I like Billy very much."

"Wow. What's that like?" she asked him.

"It's miserable. I think about him all the time. I joined the basketball team because of him. I see him flirting with girls and I get jealous. I want him to like me, too, but I know he doesn't. I want to tell him how I feel, but I am afraid it would ruin his life."

Crystal put a hand on his forearm. "Don't tell him, whatever you do. You think it's bad now? No, you don't want to tell Billy that you like him. But wow, you told me. That's pretty courageous, Lee."

"You are not like them. You are my friend. When no one would even look at me, you sat with me and talked to me. I think *that* was pretty courageous."

"I thought it was bad not liking anyone in this school. I never thought about what it would be like for me to like a girl." Crystal shook her head and stared out the window.

"You won't tell anyone?" asked Lee.

"Of course not. I was just curious. I mean, I thought there had to be a reason you didn't deny it. That would have been the logical thing to do, that first day in the gym."

"I didn't give him that note, Crystal," he said.

"I know you didn't. I always knew you didn't do that," she said.

"How did you know?"

"I can't tell you, but I knew it wasn't you."

Lee put his head in his hands, as if it were too heavy, as if he had to hold it up. "I don't understand how people can hate me so much when they don't even know me. Back in Thailand, my friends were just my friends, and almost everybody was friendly."

"Yeah, well, people are hard to figure out. I never lived in Thailand, but back in Boston, it's like that. I see the same people, just coming in and going out, at the bus stop, stores, whatever, and they may not know my name, but they say, "Hey," and "Wazzup?" and it's just no big deal. Around here, it seems *everything* is a big deal if you don't look like everybody else."

They sat in silence for a while, just staring out at nothing in particular. It was an easy silence, though, for Crystal. She never thought she'd have something in common with someone born in another country—heck, in another part of the world. Lately, Crystal felt more comfortable talking to Lee than she ever had with Tawana, even back when they were friends. How could that be?

Lee didn't seem to hold anything back. If she

asked him a question — anything, really — he'd try to answer it truthfully. Crystal found that refreshing. It's the way her family was, at least her parents. She always thought Asian people were standoffish and quiet. Lee definitely was quiet. But she liked the way he was with people — respectful, always listening, never interrupting. Still, if he had something to say, he would speak up. She admired that.

She admired more than that, if she were honest with herself. He was taller than a lot of the other seventh-grade boys. His shoulders were broad, and his hair was always clean and shiny. He dressed pretty well, considering he wasn't born here. And his skin was clear, too. That was a definite plus in the seventh grade.

Crystal didn't like it when the kids teased her. She didn't know if she liked him like that, like a boyfriend. Before she met him, she didn't like any boy at all, except her older cousins. They were fun, and she liked kidding with them. But most boys her own age were either dumb, short, or mean. If they liked to read books, it wasn't the same kind of stuff she read. The really smart boys liked to play those complicated computer games, where you took over countries or planets and had to figure out strategies. She was definitely not interested in that.

But Lee actually liked talking about things and sharing what was the same and what was different about their two cultures, Thai and American. He had a good relationship with his parents, too. That's something Crystal hadn't been able to share with a friend her own age in a long time. Everyone seemed to hate their parents, or think they were a bother. Crystal didn't know what she'd do without her mother's encouragement. She counted on their cuddling time as much today as when she was in second grade. Her mom was a rock, and her dad was the best. They did a lot of things together.

Lee once told her she was lucky to have a host family in Gilmore. "I wish my parents could talk to other parents, American parents. Sometimes they give me more homework if they don't think I have enough assigned from school."

"You're serious?" asked Crystal. "That's awful!"

"They mean well. They want me to get into a good college. They want me to do well. They say that American children are spoiled, and they're not going to let that happen to me."

"My mom thinks Gilmore kids are spoiled, too, and they are!" she said, her eyes wide open for emphasis. They both laughed at that.

Chapter Nine

One day early in November, Ms. Jones brought up a new idea to the group having lunch in her tiny office. "What do you think of starting a diversity club like they have in the high school right here?" she asked them.

"Won't work," said Tawana.

"Well, that's being positive," said Ms. Jones.

"Okay, it positively won't work," Tawana said, smiling.

"Let's at least hear the woman out," said Denisha. "What do you have in mind?"

"It's not really for me to say. The point is for you guys to form a club that would work for you," she said. Ms. Jones sat up in her chair, all five feet of her looking behind her teacher's desk just like a judge in her chambers. All she needed was a gavel.

"We're not mature enough for that," said Derek.

"Speak for yourself," said Crystal. "Who would this club be for? I mean, is it just another name for the COMBOS kids?"

"Who would you want to be a part of it?" Ms. Jones asked.

"We're not the only diversity at Gilmore," said Crystal. "We have a minority group of Asian students, too."

"What's the point of having a diversity group if only the minority groups are a part of it?" asked Denisha. "From what I'm learning, nothing changes until the majority has a change of mind and heart. Right, Ms. Jones?"

"What do you think is needed more," asked

Ms. Jones, "A club where people could come to talk about their issues of being one of the few African Americans here, or a place where people could educate the entire school about their culture?"

"You mean, we could have an assembly or some kind of event and plan it during club time?" asked Crystal.

"That's an idea."

"Just don't make it on Martin Luther King Day, please," said Derek. "It's bad enough having to sit through another 'I Have a Dream' speech with everybody peeking at us from the corner of their eyes to see if we're appreciating their once-a-year effort."

"No one would come except COMBOS kids. Who are we kidding?" said Tawana.

"Maybe if we invited our host families," said Denisha. "I think mine would come."

"It would have to be mandatory. Everyone or no one," said Tawana.

"We don't have to decide everything today, do

we?" asked Crystal.

"No, as a matter of fact, I just wanted to see if there was any interest in a club like this at all," said Ms. Jones. "The last thing I need is one more thing to chaperon."

They all laughed. Ms. Jones made no bones about how put-upon she felt sometimes as the only black teacher in the school. Try as they said they did, Gilmore couldn't seem to hold onto African American teachers for more than a year. Every time COMBOS needed something, Ms. Jones was called on. Every time a teacher had a behavior problem with a student of color, Ms. Jones was expected to mediate. Luckily, she was good at it.

"This was actually the superintendent's idea, you know," she told them.

"You're kiddin'!"

"No way!"

"I believe it," said Denisha. "Have you ever talked to Mr. Dane? He's a real thinker. I mean, he shows up at political rallies, benefits for domestic violence. He's been to every COMBOS gathering held in Roxbury since he came here to Gilmore . My mother has a lot of respect for him, and so do I."

"But he's so...white!" said Tawana, bursting out laughing.

"Well, he can't help that," Denisha said with a smile. "But he tries, he really does."

"I'm hoping you'll talk to your parents about this idea, see what they think. But more than anything, I want it to help you while you're here. Putting on a big event for the school, an assembly, is a good goal, but it may be too big a goal for this year. Maybe you'll want to start smaller."

"But if we don't do something soon, I'll be gone before it ever gets off the ground," said Denisha.

"Now is the only time we've got. You tell us that all the time, Ms. Jones," said Crystal.

"You know I hate to hear my own advice coming back at me."

"I thought you'd be glad to know we're paying attention," said Crystal.

There was an energy, a vitality in the room that had been missing an hour before. Crystal wasn't sure what made the difference. Maybe it was having something big to do, something to look forward to. She started to see this assembly as the chance she'd always wanted to teach white people a thing or two about her own tribe—not to rub their noses in it, but to show them what they were missing by not understanding, by not trying to understand. How this club would accomplish that was a question for later.

All the way back to Boston's neighborhoods on the bus, the voices of 40 or so COMBOS kids would rise and fall in waves of excitement, often brought down low by the hugeness of their task. How would you share with eleven hundred students some basics about humanity that they didn't even know they didn't know?

And how would their fellow students react to it? Crystal wanted a good outcome. She wanted more good will, not more resentment and arrogance. It wouldn't be easy. None of them was naïve enough to think it would be.

When the bus got quiet — and it did, several times — it was not the usual bored waiting-for-their-stop kind of quiet, but a thoughtful, reflective, collective, "Hmmm."

Chapter Ten

Crystal couldn't wait to talk to Lee the next day about the diversity club idea. "What do you think? Would you want to join?" she asked him.

"I don't know," he said. "Would I be the only Asian there? Would I be the only other minority besides African Americans?"

"I would hope not, but if you joined, maybe other people would, too."

"It sounds interesting. Let me think about this."

"What's to think about? Come on, you know me and Tawana and Derek, 'cause we're all on the same team," Crystal said.

"I would not call Tawana and Derek my friends," Lee said.

"I'm just saying, you know people already."

"Knowing them and liking them are two different things."

"This would be a great way for you to make new friends, Lee. Trust me on this. I know COMBOS kids. They would give you a lot of credit for joining this club. It takes a lot of guts."

"Maybe, maybe not."

Crystal was surprised that Lee was not excited about this idea. In her mind, it would be good for everybody. "What do you mean?" she asked him.

"Crystal, did you forget that just a few weeks ago I was known as the faggot of the school? Because I have not forgotten. Maybe your friends would not want someone like me joining this club."

Crystal had not given Lee's sexual orientation much thought since that time they'd discussed it.

She thought the major difference was his almond-shaped eyes, his jet-black hair, and the golden tones of his skin — not anything that went beneath his physical appearance.

"Still, I don't think you have to worry about that," said Crystal. "I don't even think about you that way at all."

"Yes, I know, and believe me, I am grateful, but that is because you know me, you are my friend, and you like me. Those other students who ride on the bus with you, they do not know me, even if we are all on the B Team. And they don't want to know me."

"Well, if that's not the point of a diversity club, I don't know what is," said Crystal. She made up her mind to bring this up at their very next meeting — or before that, if possible.

She got her chance after school that afternoon. Ever since the cafeteria incident, Tawana and Derek had taken to sitting together on the COMBOS bus. Crystal usually found a seat somewhere near them, either in a seat on the other side of the aisle, or directly in front of or behind them. On this day, she sat behind them so she could talk without turning around.

"I think I've found my first non-COMBOS member for the diversity club," she said.

"Really? Who?" asked Derek.

"Lee."

"Lee? Gay Lee?" Derek said.

"No way," said Tawana.

"Why not?" asked Crystal.

"Because I don't want to be associated with one of them, and I don't want our club to get associated with them," said Tawana.

"Listen," Derek said. "You let one of them in, and it's not a diversity club anymore. It's a gay club. That's what the one at the high school has turned into. They're using the rainbow posters, it's a freak show. We want our diversity club to be something we all can be proud of."

"Those rainbows are our symbol, too, you know," Crystal said. "Haven't you heard about the Rainbow Coalition?"

"Yeah, well looks like they've stolen it, haven't they?" said Derek.

"Look, Crystal, if you bring this up with Ms. Jones, I'm gonna be against it. It's against God, against the Bible, against our religion, and there must be some kind of school rule about it, too," said Tawana.

"Since when were you so big on staying on the right side of the rules, Tawana? You're a hypocrite, if you ask me."

"Don't go callin' me a hypocrite. I'm tellin' you I don't want any part of a club that's gonna have your friend Lee as a member."

Crystal scrunched her mouth up and jutted out her jaw. "I think that's pretty interesting. If we can't accept Lee because he's different, then what are we pretending to be doing? Don't you get it?" said Crystal.

"What I get is I don't know you anymore. I used to know you. We used to be friends. But the way your mind works is messed up, Crystal. That's what I get." Tawana turned her back on Crystal and faced the front of the bus.

"Maybe we weren't the friends I thought we were," said Crystal, to the back of Tawana's head. "I feel the same about you, Tawana. You're changing, too, and I don't know how you can do the things you do these days and be the way you are. I can't believe how different you are."

Tawana threw up her hand as if swatting a fly away. "Whatever," she said.

The two girls just sat there, not looking at each other. Crystal's mouth tried on some words, but no sound came out. So they kept quiet, and the bus roared its way through familiar streets and sights, and Crystal wondered what she could do to break the silence. The longer it continued, the harder it was to say anything.

When Tawana got up to get off at her stop, Crystal looked up. She would have said good-bye if Tawana had looked at her, but as it was, Tawana just walked off the bus without a word. It felt wrong not to say something, but...

She got home at the usual time and watched television for a while, just to chill out. Her sister got home a few minutes after she did, and they rummaged around in the kitchen cabinets for snacks, finally settling on peanut butter crackers and apple juice. Crystal sat and stared at the TV, not even registering what the show was. She kept replaying that scene on the bus and how stubborn Tawana was being. She hated to encourage Lee to join a club that would be openly hostile to him, a diversity club that was closed to a certain kind of person. She shook her head in disbelief.

Her mom had left a note on the fridge, asking her to take the lasagna pan out of the refrigerator and put it in the oven as soon as she got home. Uh oh.

Crystal was so preoccupied she didn't see the note until she went back for more apple juice. Now it was already 5:30. Dinner would be delayed, and it was her fault. She hurried to get the baking dish into the oven, setting it at a higher temperature, hoping that would take care of the half-hour lag time.

A short while later, she heard the sound of her mother's footsteps coming up the stairs.

"Mom!" she said. "I thought you'd never get here. I've got a major problem, and I don't know what to do. Will you help me?" Crystal didn't notice how tired her mother looked, her shoulders slumped, her eyelids heavy, her eyes a little bloodshot, until she was almost on top of her. "Here, let me help you with your things," she said. She took her mom's coat and hung it up on the coat rack, put her purse — spilling over with Oprah's magazine and today's mail — on the counter. Crystal's mom put in a long day, too, and was often a little winded at the top of the stairs.

"Thanks, Honey. What a ride home! The trains were stopped for the longest time, and no one said a word about why. Then they started up again, and still no explanation. That meant more people waiting at the bus stop than usual. Oh well, I'm home now. Did you remember to put the lasagna in?"

"Yes, but I didn't see the note right away. I turned the oven up to 425 though."

"You what?" she asked, rushing over to the oven and turning it down. She pulled the door down and peered inside. "You don't just do that, Crystal. Now the bottom will be burned and the middle undercooked."

"I'm sorry, Mom. I thought it would cook it faster."

"Never mind. It's hard to ruin lasagna. I can't deal with this right now. We'll just have a crispy one tonight. But I better not hear one word of complaint about dinner," she said.

Crystal made a mental note to warn her father

and sister about that one. It was her fault, after all.

"Now, if I can just free these poor feet of mine from their torture chambers," she said as she kicked off the high heels she'd been wearing all day. "I"m going to sit down and relax a minute, and then I want to hear what you want to talk to me about, but first I've got to take a few deep breaths and let all that crazy commuting stuff go." She ambled over to the living room and sank her solid, compact body into her favorite spot on the couch, lifting her feet onto the ottoman that was always right on her end.

Crystal followed her mother, eager to seize the exact moment when she would be ready to listen to her, trying not to be too pesky. Her mother hated it when she crowded her in moments like these. Crystal was trying to learn from the cues she'd been watching all her life, but it was hard. In younger days, whining and pestering her mother worked pretty well. It wasn't until the last year or so that she noticed there were other techniques, newer strategies, that would give her not only her mom's attention, but positive attention.

One of her mom's favorites was a shoulder rub, once her feet were up. Crystal came up behind the couch now, and started applying firm but gentle pressure to her mother's neck, shoulders, and upper back, right between the shoulder blades. She smiled as she heard her mother sighing.

"That is just what the doctor ordered after the day I've had," she said, smiling at her eldest child with both face and voice. "Now, just what is it you want from me?"

"Do I have to want something to be nice to my mom at the end of a long work day?"

Crystal's mom spent her days behind the customer service desk at Russell's Basement in downtown Boston, perhaps the busiest department store in the city. Some nights her mother shared stories of customers who tried to return clothing they had obviously worn and sometimes even laundered already, people who lied right through their teeth, claiming they'd just taken the tag off by mistake an hour before. Crystal's favorite was shoe returns, where shoes had been scuffed and obviously worn outside. One shoe even had dog dirt on one heel!

Crystal gave the shoulder massage another couple of minutes, more like a couple more breaths, and then came around and sat next to her mom on the couch.

"Ms. Jones asked if we wanted to start a diversity club at school. It's not a guaranteed thing, but she told us to think about it, talk to you guys and to each other, and next time we meet as a group, we're going to decide together."

"A diversity club? Just what would that be like?" her mom asked.

"We can make it anything we want it to be. That's the best part! But already there are problems. I mean, diversity, that means differences, right? And tolerance, and understanding, and making room for being the way you are. Right?" asked Crystal.

"Yes, I suppose so," her mom said.

"Well, I said I was afraid that if we didn't open it up beyond COMBOS kids, we'd only have kids just like us in the club, and how diverse is that? But when I suggested letting Asian kids into the club, Tawana and Derek said they wouldn't join a club that had Lee as a member."

"Why don't they like Lee?" she asked.

"Because Lee got into a fight, no not really. What happened is, earlier this year, Billy—you know Billy—well, someone put a note in his locker and signed it with Lee's name. The note said he liked Billy. So now the whole school thinks Lee is gay, and I'm practically the only non-Asian friend he has, and even the other Asian kids aren't being all that friendly with him."

"That's terrible. Did they ever find out who really wrote that note?"

"Well, that's not the issue anymore. See, Lee told

me he really probably *is* gay."

"Oh."

"Not that that should mean anything. I mean, he really does like Billy, but he never wrote that note, and he didn't even hit him back, even though he's a lot bigger than Billy. I just think it's rotten that people did that, and that Lee has to go around like an outcast just because someone decided to be mean to him. Plus, I think a diversity club should make room for people of different sexual orientations, too."

"So," said Crystal's mom, "What you're telling me is Tawana and Derek don't object to his being Asian but that he's gay."

"Yes, that's exactly it. And they don't even know for sure that he is. I mean, I'm his friend and he told me, but they're just going on rumors and stuff. I mean it's not like he's going to wear a sign that says, 'I'm in the diversity club because I'm gay.' People could think it's just that he's a tolerant human being who knows how hard it is to be different, being Asian in a white-dominated school like Gilmore. He's told me he thinks I'm lucky to be in COMBOS because we ride on a bus together every day and we have Ms. Jones to talk to about things. He and the other foreign-born kids don't have that."

"You certainly are invested in this, Crystal."

"Mom, what do you think about gays?" she asked.

"I haven't thought about it all that much, Honey. I mean, I know some people who are gay, of course, but I don't think I have a strong opinion, one way or the other."

"But our church does, doesn't it?"

"Well, Reverend Richard is a pretty progressive pastor, but he hasn't come out strongly for gays. He does a lot of work with people with AIDS, no matter what their gender or sexuality, but in our community, it seems to me more about IV drug use than sexual partners. But maybe I'm wrong about that, too."

"Lee is the first person I've ever known who admits he likes people of the same sex. I think he's really interesting. Derek teases me and thinks I like him, like a boyfriend, but I don't think so. I just really like him, and he's smart, and we talk about all kinds of things."

"I used to like someone and found out later he was gay," her mom said. "He was my very first love, I think. I mean, I had lots of crushes on boys, but Bradley was special. He really liked me, and we didn't play games with each other. I thought we were too good of friends to be dating, but he said he really liked me that way."

"But he turned out to be gay?"

"We went out in our senior year of high school," she said. "Then we broke up, and he went away to college, and I stayed around here. By the time he moved back to Boston, I had met your father. I didn't hear about him until it was too late. He died of AIDS a few years ago. That's when people told me.

"Wow," said Crystal. "Your first love died already?"

"Yeah, it's a sobering thought. Makes me want to make the most of today, I'll tell you."

"Mom, how would you feel if your best friends didn't want Bradley to join the diversity club because they were afraid his being in it would spoil the reputation of the club?"

"Oh honey, it's hard to think about such a thing as a diversity club existing when I was a girl. This is your world. I can hardly relate to such a thing."

"But you're not against it, are you?"

"Is this anything like a gay/straight alliance? I've heard of those groups in high schools, but not in middle schools. I'm not sure I like the idea of that kind of thing for kids your age."

"What kind of thing? Since when is diversity something you have to be fourteen or fifteen to understand or appreciate? I say the sooner we start theses things, the better."

"I know how you want me to feel about this, Crystal, but I'm going to have to think about it a little more. Talk to your dad, too. Just give me some time to ponder this a while."

"Well, I wish you'd hurry up, because I don't know what to say to Tawana tomorrow, and you know she's gonna have some fresh ammunition on the bus."

Chapter Eleven

Tossing and turning that night in her bed, Crystal finally stopped trying to fall asleep. There were only so many times you could look at the clock. So many times you could turn a pillow over to get a fresh cool patch of pillowcase against your cheek. So many sheep or ceiling tiles you could count before driving yourself crazy.

She got out of bed, put on her bathrobe, tying the sash snugly, and reached for the journal that she was now keeping under her mattress. She opened the bedroom door as quietly as she could (but it still squeaked), and she slipped out of her room.

No one was awake at 1:34 a.m., not in her house, and she was not sure how she felt about that. It was nice to have the living room all to herself, no television noise for a change. But it was a little creepy, too. She settled into her father's La-Z-Boy recliner. It lifted up your legs and feet if you leaned back into it. Holding her favorite purple gel pen in one hand and curling up her knees just right, she wrote in her journal as if she were writing on a desk. With each word and phrase, she began to empty out the thoughts that kept making their way inside her head, as monotonous and relentless as a subway car riding the rails of the Orange Line.

October 28th

It's late, and I should be asleep, but I can't let myself relax. I want to jump out of my bed and do something about this diversity club, and I want to do it right now! There must be something I can do or say to make people like Derek and Tawana understand. If I can't convince them how important it is to let a nice kid like Lee into our club, how will we ever convince the other kids at Gilmore that we're people, too? I see it all as the same thing. Why don't they? Why do they have to feel better than Lee? He never did anything to them. It's frustrating to see something so clearly and not be able to change their minds about it. It's not like they don't know how it feels. They do. So why are they doing the same thing to someone else? I don't get it. I will never get it. What's so hard for them to understand about this?

She sighed, put down her pen, and wandered around the living room, looking at some of her family's most treasured possessions. Her dad had gone to Africa before he married Crystal's mom and came back with some sculptures and a few tapestries made by African artists and weavers. He told her how that visit to Africa changed his whole life, changed how he felt about himself. He said he never saw the world exactly the same way again.

Something about so many black people—*everywhere*—from people walking on the streets to people who owned the stores and the people who ran the villages. He said there were black people wherever you looked! He didn't feel strange or out of place or different, even though he was an American. He felt like he belonged there, that he was at home, safe, just like everyone else.

Crystal imagined that's how Lee must have felt in Thailand and then wondered if being gay might take that feeling of belonging away from him. She wondered how much tolerance there was for gays where he came from, and whether he would follow the traditional path his parents expected him to follow and marry a Thai girl when he was old enough to do that.

Crystal looked at the clock again: 2:49. This

was not good. She had a long day ahead of her, and being tired before school started was a horrible way to begin. Even if she had a full eight hours of sleep, Crystal usually felt tired because she had to get up so early, but she couldn't remember the last time her thoughts had kept her awake so long.

She went into the kitchen, poured herself a glass of milk, drank it down, and rinsed out the glass. Her mom said that sometimes a little milk at night is all her stomach needed to ease her into sleep mode. She hoped it would work tonight.

When morning came, Crystal realized she must have slept, because she woke up with a start to her alarm clock at 5 a.m. She couldn't believe she really had to get out of bed.

"Crystal? Was that you I heard padding around in the wee hours last night?" her mom asked.

"I couldn't sleep. I'm telling you, Mom, my head is so full I thought it would explode if I left it on that pillow a minute longer. I just got up and walked around a little, wrote in my journal, and had some milk."

"Did that help?"

"I guess so. But I couldn't have slept more than two hours."

"Well, maybe when you come home you can take a nap," her mom said.

"Oh yeah, like that's gonna happen," Crystal said.

"If you hunkered down as soon as you got home..." her mother began.

"Not likely. I'll make up the sleep on the weekend," she said.

"So what did you come up with?"

"Nothing. Absolutely nothing. I'm just going to keep my opinions to myself on the bus and wait to discuss it when Ms. Jones is around. Otherwise, I don't know what I'll do or say, but I'll probably regret it."

"Good thinking," her mom said.

✳ ✳ ✳

That day she fell asleep on the bus going to school. After all that worry, neither Tawana nor Derek said a word to her. They just let her sleep. In homeroom and all that morning, Crystal's eyelids took longer and longer to blink as the hands on the clock slowly, slowly made their way around. She didn't remember much about her classes or even lunch. She was there but not there, suffering from sleep deprivation.

On the way up the stairs from the cafeteria, though, she overheard some kids talking, and the way they were huddled around each other, she knew something big was up. She tried to move closer without being too obvious about wanting to hear their conversation. She didn't look at them and kept her eyes on the steps and her feet, but her attention was keenly focused on listening to the snippets of their conversation. One said, "I heard her crying in the bathroom stall next to me, even before homeroom."

Another said, "They really called her Annie Rexic and said she was as ugly as a dyke?"

"I heard she didn't even make it to first period. And you know what a grade-grubber she is."

"She's not a grade-grubber. She's just smart."

Who were they talking about? She didn't have to wait long to find out. Tawana and Derek were head to head in English class by the time Crystal got there. They stopped talking when they saw Crystal walk in. She knew they were part of this one, too.

She looked away from them — as if she couldn't care less what they were talking about — slid into her seat, and pulled out her notebook and folder for this class. She wrote in the date, looked up at the white board for homework assignments, and sat patiently, waiting for Ms. Levantov to start the class.

"Look! There she is!" Derek said, trying to whisper but too excited to contain himself.

Crystal looked in that direction and saw what must have been their victim of the day. Sally's tall, skinny frame was hunching over an armful of books. The clothes she wore, several sizes too big, were designed to hide her thinness, but if you looked at her from the side, she practically disappeared. Today her eyes were red and swollen, probably from crying, and she looked more fragile than ever. Sally was one of the smartest kids on the B Team and had always been thin. But this year, since school began, her weight was dropping fast. Was she really anorexic, Crystal wondered, or sick from some terrible disease? Her hair, once blond and shiny, was very, very thin and sparse, and you could see through to the top of her head.

Not a trace of makeup colored her complexion, which was gray these days. Crystal tried to make eye contact with Sally as she walked by her desk and took her own seat, but Sally kept her head down and didn't see the attempt at friendliness.

The truth was, she and Sally were not friends. They hardly knew each other. It was unusual for her to come late to class, to draw attention to herself in any way at all. Crystal tried not to stare, but everyone was looking in Sally's direction.

Crystal turned around to see if Tawana and Derek were gloating, but they looked more sheepish now than anything else. On the way home on the bus, Crystal couldn't wait to ask. She had to know.

"Tell me you didn't write another note for them, Tawana," she said. "I know they did it, and I know it was Sally, from the look on her face. But please tell me you, at least, didn't have any part of it this time."

"What do you know about anything?" said Tawana.

"I know what it looks like when you think everyone is against you. And Sally had that look on today. And I know that you did it before, to Lee. I hope it's not true, but I think, yeah, you could have done it again."

"Well, I didn't write that note," she said, but she couldn't look Crystal in the eye.

Crystal kept staring at her, and Tawana kept looking down.

"Are you scared of them? That maybe they'll turn on you if you don't do what they say?" Crystal seemed satisfied, finally, and said, as if to herself, "Why else would you be making school miserable for people who have a hard enough time as it is?"

Tawana lifted up her head a notch. "It just seemed like a joke at the time."

"What did the note say?"

"I don't remember it, exactly. Something about Dear Annie Rexic, you're so ugly, how can you stand looking at yourself in the mirror? Something like that."

"Well, what I heard was you called her a lesbo or a dyke. And anyway, what if she can't help it? I doubt she's starving herself on purpose."

"Yes, she is," said Derek. "Did you ever see her tray in the cafeteria? She takes one little bowl of applesauce and maybe a tiny salad, and that's it. She *wants* to look like that! We were just trying to let her know she's gone too far, that's all."

"Tawana, this has got to stop," said Crystal. "Did you ever stop to think how you would feel if someone did that to you?"

"People *do* do that to me. Remember? That's what this school is like. I'm not going to change it. Suzanne even said it's happened to her. She told me that when her parents got divorced last year, someone kept calling her on the phone and telling her stuff about her dad. Said her father was sleeping around, and that's why he was leaving town and taking a job in New York. She says every time she comes up with another hate-note idea, it makes her feel a little better. She had to get over it, and so will they."

Crystal sat back and took a deep breath. Every one of the kids Tawana was now hanging around with probably had a story like this. They weren't really the cool kids. They weren't on the soccer team or the honor roll. Their parents made a lot of money, maybe, but these kids were struggling, too, in their own way. She had never seen that before. Maybe that was why they skipped school and did stupid things.

When Crystal leaned forward to talk to Tawana again, it wasn't with an angry voice. "It wasn't right what you did, Tawana. You know that, don't you?"

"Yeah," she said. "But what can I do about it now? It's done."

The two girls sat deep in thought as the bus rumbled on its way, passing the Dunkin' Donuts, a used-car lot, and the long row of stores selling everything from futons to guitars as they went through Boston University apartment buildings. This was the slowest part of the ride.

"You could say you're sorry," Crystal finally said.

"I can't do that! I'd get kicked out of school if I admitted to writing that note," she said.

Crystal sighed in agreement. But she wasn't sure. Maybe Tawana should get turned in or should turn herself in. Maybe it would take some big gesture like that to make everyone see that it had to stop.

Suddenly she sat bolt upright in her seat. "I know! I know what will fix this!" she said.

"What?" Tawana asked. "Come on, girl, tell me what you're thinking!"

"Well, writing that note is what got you into this mess, right? So write a note of apology to get you out of it. But I don't mean the kind you say to a teacher. I mean a really heartfelt apology, delivered the same way this one was, in the same handwriting — yours."

"I could do that," Tawana said, her face brightening for the first time since they'd started talking.

"I'll help if you want," said Crystal.

"No, I'll do it myself, but maybe you could look it over when I'm done?"

"Sure."

It was decided, then. Crystal was relieved. She felt good about getting through to Tawana, good about understanding everything a little better.

For the first time in a long time, it felt good to be friends with Tawana again.

Chapter Twelve

The next morning, Tawana took the note out of her backpack as soon as she sat down next to Crystal on the bus. "Here it is," she said. "What do you think?"

Crystal unfolded the note and read it carefully:

Dear Sally,

You don't know me, and I really don't know you very well. I'm the one who wrote that note yesterday. If I had known how bad it would make you feel, I never would have done it. It was a practical joke, a stupid,

*mean thing to do, and I'm sorry. I'll never write
another note like that to you or anybody, ever again.
I'm sorry it made you cry.*

"Wow, Tawana, that's pretty good," said Crystal, carefully folding the note and handing it back. "No, I mean it. It's really a good note."

"I hope so. That's the third or fourth version of it. I kept crossing things out and adding things in. My conscience was really bothering me."

"That's what a conscience is for," said Crystal. "If it doesn't stop us from acting stupid, at least it tries to stop us from enjoying what we did. So, are you ready to discuss this diversity club thing again?"

"Oh Crystal, not again."

"I'm not gonna let up until you change your mind, Tawana. This is important to me. Maybe more important because Lee and I are becoming friends. But I've been trying really hard to under-stand why you're against this, and it just doesn't make any sense to me."

"I'm not as good at explaining things as you are," she said. "It just feels wrong to me. I think us COMBOS kids have a hard enough time trying to be accepted and looked at as just as good as everyone else here at Gilmore. I think it will be harder for us if we start letting gays into this club."

"How could it be any worse? Some of them already think we're not quite human. And maybe, just maybe, if lots of different kids come into the club, we could stretch the idea out about diversity. I mean, there's no reason it has to be just differences about what we look like or where we were born or what language we speak. Maybe even Suzanne might want to join."

"What? I thought you hated Suzanne."

"If this club is going to work, it can't be something we exclude people from for any reason. So what if I don't like her? I really don't know her very well, and what you told me about her yesterday helps me understand her a little bit. It can't be easy to watch your parents go through a divorce, to have your dad move away to another state."

"I doubt she'd want to join," said Tawana.

"Maybe not, but we could invite her. What if this club helped everybody stop judging from what we seem like on the outside and really helped us to know each other from the inside? I mean what's the point of having a club with a new name that's just the same kids we ride the bus with day in and out?"

"You've definitely got a point there," said Tawana. "This is a whole new way to think about the diversity club."

Crystal felt better already. Now if only Derek would come on board, they'd really be getting somewhere. Derek had a big mouth, and when he said something in that comical way he had, people would go along with him.

"Would you talk about this to Derek for me?"

she asked Tawana.

"No, but I'd talk to Derek *with* you."

✳ ✳ ✳

When the COMBOS kids met with Ms. Jones a week later, Crystal was ready. She and Tawana had asked their health teacher for the statistics she had put together for them about gay and lesbian teens, the ways school wasn't safe for them, the higher rates of drinking, drugs, smoking, and suicide, and Crystal held that paper in her hand tightly. She wasn't sure when or how she would need those facts, but something about the power of those numbers made her confident she could change a few minds. She felt certain that enough of the kids who were opposed to having Lee in the club would come around and see it differently.

"Well," Ms. Jones said, "I hope you've had time to think about the diversity club idea, and I just want to say that nothing we say here has to happen right away. We're just beginning to explore this idea, and I'm looking forward to hearing your thoughts about it since we first discussed it. Who wants to go first?"

No one spoke for an awkward moment or two. They were just looking at each other. Derek spoke up first. "What I like about it is the idea that we could finally say some things to the majority of kids here at Gilmore that we've been just saying to ourselves, 'cause I'm really sick of talking to myself. Nothing changes that way."

"I agree with that," said an eighth grader. "I also think we could have fun putting an assembly together that has a little life in it, you know? Most of the ones we have here are so boring!"

"Plus, I don't know, maybe what we do could help COMBOS kids who come along after us," said Denisha. "I'm glad to be here at Gilmore. I'm getting a really solid education, and I know I'll be happy to graduate from this school system and get into a good college. But it's hard, a lot of the time, just dealing with simple prejudice and ignorance. I'd like to find a way to make my experience here benefit someone else. That way, it wouldn't be wasted."

Crystal raised her hand to speak, quietly but firmly. "I feel strongly that we should open this club up to any kind of diversity we have in this school, and also to anyone who wants to learn more about diversity. So basically, I'm saying anyone should be able to join this club."

"If we really mean that everyone should be treated with respect, then that should mean everyone," said Tawana, her face flushed from speaking in front of the group in this way.

Derek couldn't restrain himself. "Tawana, are you agreeing with Crystal all of a sudden? What's goin' on? I thought we had an understanding about this."

"We did, but then I got to thinking about it, and now I understand what Crystal is saying. I mean, we can't force people to want to join, but I think we should welcome everyone who feels like an outsider in this school, or anyone who wants to learn about different kinds of people."

Ms. Jones interrupted by leaning forward into the circle. "What kinds of outsiders are you thinking about, Crystal and Tawana?"

"Well, there are some gay and lesbian kids who go to Gilmore, and Asian kids, and Armenian, Iraqi—heck, there are a lot of little mini-groups and people of different religions. I think this should be a club that's open to everyone, especially people who feel like they don't belong."

"If we opened it up to all the mini-groups, we might be a majority," said Derek, half joking.

"You know that might be an interesting way to approach it," said Ms. Jones. "What if there are more people at Gilmore who feel like they don't belong than people who feel like they do?"

"I mean, at Christmas time, how do the Jewish kids feel? And at Ramadan how do the Muslim kids feel when they just sit there at lunch while everyone else is wolfing down pizza?" said Denisha.

"Then there are the poor white kids who live in the projects. You can't tell me they feel like they're in the majority," Tawana piped up again.

"Yeah, and the kids who have to go to the Resource Center for extra help with homework because of their learning disabilities," said Devon, who almost never spoke.

"What about Matthew—you know, the kid in the wheelchair?" Denisha said.

The more the kids talked about it, the more energy and excitement filled the room. Ms. Jones sat back, pleased at the turn this was taking. "I don't know, you guys. This is a big picture we're looking at. How are we going to let people know what we mean when we say the diversity club?"

Suddenly, Crystal noticed the statistical report she held in her hand. Maybe someday in the near future, they could use these numbers when educating their fellow students about how to make schools safer for gay and lesbian kids, but she didn't need that piece of paper today. She put the paper in her backpack and smiled over at Tawana. They got it. This motley crew of kids bused in from Boston, her group, they got it. She was happy.

Ms. Jones brought the easel over with the newsprint pad so they could write down all their brainstorming ideas for introducing this new club to the school community: weekly PA announcements about the club; fun facts about different minority groups represented here at Gilmore; snacks and international food suppers; art exhibits; and world music played in the cafeteria during lunchtime. There were so many ways to bring differences to light and make people more familiar with them.

"What are we gonna call this club?" someone yelled out. "Diversity club doesn't really sound right."

Ms. Jones ripped off a fresh piece of newsprint. "I'm going to pass this one around and ask you all to write something, anything, that comes to mind. It could be a word, a phrase, a name, but it doesn't have to be a name. Just write the first thing that comes to you, or something that inspires you from what other people wrote. I'd like us to be really quiet until the paper is passed all the way around the room."

A purple magic marker was handed from person to person along with the newsprint. It wasn't easy to be quiet, but everyone was respecting Ms. Jones request to give people time to think.

The more that was written down, the more Crystal could feel something, like a silent wave, moving in the circle. You could almost touch it. By the time it got to Crystal, here's what she read:

Open to Everybody

What does it take to
matter around here, anyway?

Hope

Finally   Say It Now

I'm Special

Respect

All About Me and Mine

All About Us

Ask Me

Don't Assume   Just Human

Just As Human

What Did I Ever Do to You?

No More Hiding

Express Yourself

Pride

Hey — I'm HERE

Stories

Freedom   Freedom Isn't Free

Insiders & Outsiders

Inside Outsiders

When the paper was passed all the way around, Ms. Jones told everyone she'd keep it taped to her wall and add more paper if they needed more room, so that if people came into her office with a new idea, they could add it to the mix. She asked for volunteers to read what had been written, pausing between each one so the words had a chance to sink in.

When it was read completely through, she beamed at them. "See what can happen when you let yourselves think together on something? This is an amazing piece of work. I'm so proud of all of you. Let's just give it another week or so to think about all this, then we'll come back and take the next steps."

Crystal was impressed by what they had all come up with together, too. She didn't think they had it in them. Even the fifth and sixth graders were into it. She liked the feeling inside the room, different from other times when they would just gripe and complain.

That was good, too, to get it all out. But when they'd walk out of the room on those days, they wouldn't feel like things would ever get different around here.

That night Crystal wrote in her journal:

November 6th

I don't know what to call it but Hope. That's what was different about today. I feel that way in church, especially when the music's playing and everyone's singing and I can feel how big we are together. I just never felt that way inside Gilmore Middle School until today. I like it. I want to feel that way more often. This club, I don't want to get my hopes too high, but I think we could really do something important with this club.

The next day on the bus, Crystal didn't know what to expect. She was almost afraid to step up and take her seat. What if it was just like every other day?

What if the spirit inside Ms. Jones' room was just a passing mood, and now it was gone?

Crystal was just as tired as ever, but she was interested in making eye contact with people on the bus. She noticed that when someone new came on, she made it a point to say hello, when before she would have ignored them. That was different in a good way.

And she wasn't the only one.

"Hey, Tawana," she called to her friend as she climbed up on the bus.

"Hey, back at you," Tawana said, smiling.

"How are you doing today?"

"I'm doing better, Crystal. I'm feeling good."

"Me, too," said Crystal. "Me, too."

The End

Made in the USA
Middletown, DE
05 June 2015